The Librarian's Ruse

"A debut novel filled with romance, sibling rivalry, and the difficult decisions of staying true to oneself, *The Librarian's Ruse* delivers on all accounts."

Kim Catron

#1 Bestselling Author of *Threshing of Straw*

"This enchanting story drew me in and had me turning pages right to the end. The characters were a delight to get to know. I'm already looking forward to the next installment!"

Rebekah Olson

Author of *Spell Caster*

"An amazing young adult fantasy novel! *The Librarian's Ruse* is a great adventure, and Thirzah is a new author to watch!"

Brad Pauquette

Author of *Sejal: The Walk for Water*

"Both mysterious and delightful, *The Librarian's Ruse* nails the pulse of young adults craving a fantastic world of charming romance, turbulent suspense, and engaging identities."

NeShea Jenifer

Author of *PoetrEmotions*

The Librarian's Ruse

Adventures in Eldnaire
Book One

Thirzah

The Pearl

PEARLBOOKS.CO

Developmental Editor
BRAD PAUQUETTE AND MICHAYLAH MALONE

Copy Editor
ALLI PRINCE AND LINDSEY RENEE BACKEN

Cover Designer
JESSICA OSTRANDER AND BRAD PAUQUETTE

Book Design
ALLI PRINCE

Copyright © 2023 by Thirzah Griffioen

LCCN: 2023943529

Print ISBN: 978-1-960230-02-7
E-book ISBN: 978-1-960230-03-4

To Mom, Dad, and everyone else who wouldn't let me say no to my dreams. You know who you are, and I'm grateful for everything you've done.

Also, to my brother, who definitely did not inspire a character in this book, no matter what anyone else says.

Love you!

One

A shriek filled the forest. I gripped my brother's arm, eyes exploring the surrounding trees.

Several shouts echoed through the wood ahead of us. The dense foliage of the Vilnarian forest obscured part of my view, but two hooded figures dashed across the dirt road. One figure stumbled, carrying a third person—a woman. She moaned in agony as the group disappeared into the brush on the other side of the road.

My brother jerked my arm, yanking me off the road behind a large tree. I clung to the rough bark, breathing hard.

"That way!"

A man's voice. Harsh and lilting, echoed through the trees.

I looked out from our hiding place. A man sprinted across the road, followed by two other men. All three disappeared, but their feet pounded against the forest floor, snapping twigs and crushing fallen leaves.

Leon shifted next to me, reaching for the hilt of his sword.

"Don't!" I hissed up at him.

He glanced in the direction that the figures had fled. His shoulders tensed. "I can help."

I grasped his arm. "No, you can't!"

Leon snorted, yanking his arm away. "Watch me." He stepped out from behind the tree, hand returning to his sword.

I rushed forward, placing my tiny frame between my brother and the road. "There's three of them, and if they all have weapons then—"

"Amelia, get out of the way."

"I can't! Leon, we're librarians, not warriors! Please, you're going to—"

Another shriek echoed throughout the forest, cutting me off. The shriek was followed by a yell before silence settled in the area once more.

My feet stayed planted on the forest floor as if I'd become a tree. My hands flew to my mouth as I stared up at Leon. He stared back, his brown eyes wide.

The leaves above us rustled in the wind as if whispering what they'd seen. Three victims, three murderers, and two witnesses who did nothing to help. Pinpricks of darkness flooded my vision. I reached for Leon's arm to steady myself, but he stepped away.

"Let's go," he muttered, brushing past me. "You wanted to make it to Eldnaire before lunch, didn't you?"

Words refused to rise to my lips. I trembled as Leon walked down the small dirt road. I joined my brother on the path, shuffling along several feet behind him.

Strands of my dark hair fell as my tight updo loosened, tickling my cheeks and the nape of my neck. I fixed my gaze upon the uneven road as we walked, keeping my ears on high alert. The bandits may have already found prey, but the slightest rustling of leaves or drop of a branch could signal that they had returned for more.

We walked for a few minutes before reaching the location where the two groups had crossed. Leon stopped, examining the forest floor. I stepped closer, peering at the ground. A trail of dark red dots stained the cracked dirt and dry leaves.

I winced, averting my gaze.

Leon bent over, picking something up from off the ground. "I see…they were mercenaries," he said, examining the small object.

He held the item out to me. I took it, turning it over. A simple brooch with brown enamel, shaped like a shield. A bright red dragon had been painted onto it. I looked up at Leon.

"A brooch?"

"Mercenaries wear these to show they're up for hire. They wear them in marketplaces and taverns or at the docks." Leon frowned, "But this brooch looks Myarnan, not Vilnarian."

I frowned. "How would you know that?"

He shrugged. "Ivan showed me a few of the different mercenary brooches after training a few months ago."

My eyes widened. "You trained with Ivan Lidare? Mother and father forbade you from having anything to do with him!"

Leon scoffed. "Well, Mother and Father tend to forget that I'm an adult and that I don't need to obey their every wish and command anymore."

He reached out to take the brooch, but I pulled it closer.

"Ivan is a murderer!"

"It's his job."

"That doesn't mean it's right!"

Leon pursed his chapped lips, frowning. "Look, he's only killed a few smugglers…it's not like he kills innocent people." He looked down at the bloodstained ground, tapping one of his brown leather boots against the leaves. "My guess is that these mercenaries were hired to kill those travelers. They were probably smugglers, too. Or worse."

I crossed my arms over my chest. "You can't know that."

"No, but I'm probably right. A lot of mercenaries are hired by governments to find and get rid of smugglers, slave-traders, and bandits."

"They're killed without a trial?" My gaze fell to the blood-covered leaves as my stomach lurched.

Leon scowled. "Scum like them don't deserve a trial. Mercenaries are just doing everyone a favor by—" he stopped, sniffing the air. "Hey, do you smell that?"

As he spoke, the overwhelming scent of charred wood filled my nose. "Fire…"

He nodded. "Looks like it. Over there."

I followed Leon's gaze. To our right, a feathery plume of smoke rose from the trees, swirling up into the sky.

"Do you think it has to do with…what happened?" I glanced down at the dragon brooch.

Leon shrugged. "Who knows? Let's check it out." He

stepped off the narrow road, into the brush.

My eyes widened. "Wait—check it out? But we need to get out of here! What if those men return?"

Leon glanced over his shoulder, patting his sword's hilt. "If anything happens, I'll protect you. Besides…Eldnaire is only about an hour from here. We'll arrive just after lunch—even if we take a little detour."

I clenched my fists, shaking my head. "Leon, please…can we just go?"

Leon sighed, running a hand through his short, wavy black hair. "Hey, look. I just want to see what's going on, okay? We'll head to Eldnaire right after."

"But Leon—" I stopped, pursing my lips. There was no point in arguing with someone who would never take no for an answer. It'd just be a waste of time. "Fine."

I shoved the brooch into the coin purse I wore around my neck as I plodded after Leon, trudging through the trees in the direction of the swirling gray smoke.

We reached our destination after about five minutes of stumbling over the bumpy forest ground. A campsite—or at least, what was left of it, sat abandoned in the middle of a small clearing. Berries, nuts, and dried meat lay scattered on the ground like chicken feed. I spotted three traveling packs by the dying fire, two of which looked as though someone had trampled them.

"No wonder those smugglers got themselves killed," Leon said, staring at the orange flames the campfire emitted. "If they didn't want to be found, they shouldn't have made a fire. It's as if they've never traveled through a forest before."

"You don't even know if they were guilty of smuggling," I muttered.

Leon must not have heard, or perhaps he simply chose to ignore me, because he didn't argue. Several birds pecked at the nuts and berries on the ground, but they flew off as we entered the camp.

Leon knelt down, inspecting one of the traveling packs. He unclasped the buckle, peering inside. His eyes widened. "Of all the—that's a lot of stuff!" A grin spread over his face. "Yeah, those people were *definitely* smugglers."

"Or innocent merchants. There's really no way to tell." I glanced back in the direction we came from—half expecting to hear leaves crunching and twigs snapping beneath a mercenary's murderous foot. "We should leave before someone comes," I murmured.

He nodded, but instead of walking back toward the road as I hoped, he began digging through one of the travelers' packs.

I blinked. "Wait, what are you doing? We—" Out of the corner of my eye, I spotted movement. I jumped, gasping as I turned. A couple of sparrows landed on the ground nearby, pecking at the berries and nuts. I let out a deep breath, placing my hand over my rapidly beating heart as I turned back to my brother who was still hunched over on the ground. "Leon, didn't you hear me? We have to go!"

Leon continued digging through the bag. He reached deep inside and pulled out what looked like a white rug, spilling various packages and jars onto the ground in the process. I stepped closer, examining it. Upon closer inspection, the rug turned out to be a fur coat.

The coat looked as though someone had caught a cloud and spun it into a fabric. Streaks of silver decorated the snow-white fur and swirling designs had been sewn on with silver thread.

The designs reminded me of the embroidered blankets our grandmother used to make for Leon and me in the winter. I reached out to touch the fur, but stopped, my fingers inches away. I dropped my hand, looking up at Leon.

"Put it back...we really need to go."

Leon nodded. "Right, of course." He tucked the coat in the crook of his arm but continued digging through the bag.

My face grew hot. I grit my teeth, clenching my fists as I shot my brother a glare. "Leon, why won't you just listen? You're going to get us killed!"

He glanced at me. "Lia, do you really think the mercenaries deserve to be rewarded for murder? Even if they were hired to kill these people?"

I frowned. "What? No, of course not!"

Leon nodded. "My thoughts exactly. But since they're already going to get paid for their work, there's not much we can do... unless we take these goods."

My mouth hung open as I stared at my older brother. "Take the—in what way does stealing make up for murder? Have you lost your mind?"

Leon shoved a couple of the wrapped packages into his bag.

"On the contrary, I'm using it."

"Leon, if we're really going to help, we should go into the city and…and inform the guards there about this. They can question the mercenaries and find out who hired them to do this."

He snorted, swatting a fly away from his face before transferring a few more packages and jars to his bag. "We're in Vilnaria. Why would Vilnarian guards care that Vilnarian mercenaries robbed and killed a few foreign smugglers? It's probably the Vilnarians who hired the mercenaries in the first place. I mean, since they love to plunder foreign land, why would they stop there?"

"Well, yes, but there haven't been any invasions in months." I frowned. "Besides…didn't you say the mercenaries had a Myarnan brooch?"

"The only reason there haven't been any wars recently is because the emperor got sick and died," Leon said. "But do you really think his son will be any different? Give it a few months and I'm sure he'll set his sights on the east—especially a wealthy city like Myarna."

I hated how clearly I could picture it. Myarna in flames as a legion of Vilnarian troops marched down the streets, establishing their new order and declaring Myarna to be part of the Vilnarian Empire.

"What does that have to do with the fact that stealing is wrong?"

"Don't think of it as stealing. We'll just be keeping this stuff safe until the original owners can claim it."

There were no words in any language I'd been acquainted with to express just how utterly ridiculous this situation was. "Leon…

surely you understand—"

"Come on, you're just wasting time," he said, pointing at one of the other traveling packs. "The sooner we do this, the sooner we can leave these woods." Leon smiled. "That's what you want, right?"

I frowned. "You're really going to do this."

Leon smirked at me as he shoveled a few more packages into his pack. "The mercenaries that you're so scared of are probably on their way back here right now, Lia. We'd better hurry."

My resolve crumbled like an ancient castle. "Fine…we'll take the stuff with us," I placed my hands on my hips, staring at Leon, "but only so we can turn it over to the proper authorities the *minute* we reach the city. Got it?"

Leon rolled his eyes. "Yeah, yeah, of course. Now hurry up and help me."

I shook my head, kneeling down beside the unknown stranger's traveling pack. Loosening the drawstrings, I reached inside, grabbing the first brown wrapped package.

The forest had seen murderers, smugglers, and now the trees stood tall and alert, watching as a brother and sister became temporary thieves.

Within a few minutes of digging and shoving items into our travel packs, Leon and I amassed quite the array of goods—including a fur cape in addition to the coat Leon had found.

Leon unwrapped a few of the packages to reveal spices, jewelry, strange dried fruit, and even decorative weapons. With our bags already filled with books and our other travel supplies, we didn't have enough room for every item.

"We could take one of the bags with us," Leon suggested.

I frowned. "Do you plan to carry it?"

Leon grimaced. "I may be strong but I'm still human... I'm already carrying most of the library books." He smirked. "Of course...we could always leave them here."

My eyes widened. "What? No! It's our duty to deliver them all in one piece to the imperial library!"

Leon sighed. "I don't see why it matters... It's not like anyone would be able to prove we didn't... But fine, fine..." He pursed his lips, studying the remaining goods. "Let's see... Hey, since the furs take up the most space, why don't we wear them?"

I pointed at my mud-brown traveling dress—purposely chosen due to its short sleeves and feather light feel—then at Leon's outfit, a short-sleeved, cream-colored tunic with a brown belt and green riding pants. "It's not exactly winter, Leon..."

He laughed, standing. "It's barely spring. We'll be fine."

Leon grabbed my hand, pulling me to my feet. He handed me the fur coat, so I slipped it on over my traveling dress.

The fur of the coat felt softer than silk against my skin. I moved my arms around within the long sleeves, pressing my lips in a firm line to keep from smiling.

"I could get used to this," Leon said, admiring the fur cape he'd just fastened around his broad shoulders.

I frowned. "Well, don't. We're turning all of this over to the guards the second we reach the city, remember?" I forced myself to look away from the bright, silvery-white fur, my eyes sweeping the surrounding forest. "Besides, these furs would be easy to spot, Leon. Even through the trees…"

"It's fine, we're going." Leon grinned, pointing up in the air in the direction of the rising sun. "Now, onward to Eldnaire!"

Two

After a full hour of walking, we finally reached the gates of Eldnaire. As we entered the crowded Vilnarian city, I walked a few steps behind Leon—a mistake I quickly remedied when several people came within inches of crashing straight into me.

Leon laughed as I grabbed his arm.

"Maybe if you were a little taller, people would actually be able to see you."

I glared up at him, "There isn't much I can do about that."

He chuckled but didn't tease me any further as we approached the city square. To our right stood the marketplace, a bustling hub of trade, conversation, and activity. A variety of smells and sounds swirled up and around us, beckoning Leon and I to explore.

"Hey, why don't we walk around for a bit?" Leon suggested, his eyes scanned the array of stalls and shops lining the marketplace.

I forced myself to shake my head, frowning. "Not until

we've reported the—incident, and turned these goods over to the guards," I said, glancing at Leon's bulky traveling pack. "You promised we'd do that first thing. Besides, we also need to deliver the library books as soon as possible!"

Leon sighed, putting his huge hand on my tiny shoulder. "Lia, we're in Eldnaire—we should be enjoying ourselves! If you're planning to spend the rest of your life holed up in that library, who knows when you'll get an opportunity like this again?"

I shrugged his hand off my shoulder, glaring. "Stop it!" I snapped. "Help me look for a guard post. We can enjoy ourselves *after* we've turned the goods over to the proper authorities." I brushed some more loose strands of hair behind my ears.

Leon glanced around, opening his mouth to respond. "Yeah, I know, but—" he stopped, gasping.

I followed his gaze. On the other end of the city square stood a large stone building with a bell tower at the top. A couple of tall wooden beams stuck up from the ground in front of it. But the structure next to it is what claimed my attention.

I'd never seen a building more extravagant than the Vilnarian palace. Not even the Hall of Justice in Myarna's city center could compare to the show of architectural genius before me. The palace looked big enough to host an army of ten thousand—at least. It stretched the length of the entire town square and beyond the marketplace. Between the white walls and gold embellishments, it literally outshone all the buildings around it in the noonday sun.

The grounds of the palace were well manicured. Red roses and shrubs shaped like winged dragons lined the stone walkways leading to the palace's entrances and exits.

"It looks like there are more windows than walls," Leon remarked, staring up at the enormous structure. "I pity the servants that have to wash them."

I nodded. "The palace could be a city in itself with all the outer buildings, the garden, and library…"

As I spoke, my attention turned toward the library. Several guards patrolled the area as a steady stream of visitors walked up and down the marble steps, entering and exiting the large, gold-trimmed wooden doors of the library's public entrance.

"That's a lot of people," I murmured.

"I bet most of them can't even read," Leon said, "they're probably just there to say they've been inside the palace."

I frowned, looking at the domed structure attached to the large, gleaming building. It didn't shine as much as the rest of the palace. The copper roof of the dome was jade-green from exposure to the elements. Instead of white walls, the library was made up of chipped gray stone, covered in a deep green curtain of ivy. "It's the largest library on the continent…over two hundred years old. It's a historical landmark."

"But who actually cares about that?" Leon pointed to the golden roofs and white walls. "The palace is the real attraction." He grinned, tilting his head. "I wonder how many people not-so-accidentally end up wandering around the palace halls while 'looking for a book.'"

I shook my head. "Only half of the library is open to the public," I said, "the other half is strictly for the use of the nobles and the imperial family."

Leon scoffed, crossing his arms over his chest. "It's no wonder. The royals can't afford for mere *peasants* to flip through the pages of their favorite dictionaries. I mean, they might actually *learn* something." He grimaced. "Now, if *I* were emperor, I'd—"

"Leon, don't be so loud," I murmured, glancing around as a few couples strolled by. "What if someone hears you?"

Leon laughed, shaking his head. "What? Are you afraid that the guards will come and—"

"Ah, here you are."

Leon and I whirled around.

A tall, red-haired man with a mustache stood there, smiling at us. He wore a dark violet cloak and carried a decorative iron cane with an amethyst stone embedded in the top.

"And...you are?" Leon asked. He spoke to the man in the short, lilting language of the Vilnarians. With Leon's light mountain accent, his words sounded melodic.

The man placed his hand across his chest, bowing. "Ah, right...my apologies. Seeing the two of you here like this made me forget my manners. I am Sir Ferdinand Richard Isaacs, at your service." He straightened, looking me in the eye, "but I would be honored if you would simply address me as Sir Fern."

My brother and I exchanged a glance.

Leon cleared his throat. "Well, Sir Fern... Thank you for the warm greeting, however, I'm afraid my sister and I have important business to attend to, so—"

Sir Fern nodded. "Yes, I am aware. In fact, it's why I'm here."

I blinked. "It is?"

He chuckled. "Yes. You are our esteemed guests after all. The emperor himself has asked me to greet you and escort you to the palace." He sighed. "Between the merchant caravans that arrived just yesterday and all the executions scheduled for this week, the emperor wanted to make sure you didn't get lost in all the crowds."

I blinked, my stomach dropping. "Executions?"

Sir Fern pursed his lips, glancing about the square. "Well, of course I don't want to worry you, but since the late emperor's death, all manner of criminals have been lurking about, believing they can get away with just about anything—murder, fraud, thievery…" he shook his head, pointing to our left. "But sooner or later they all learn that they cannot escape justice."

I followed his finger, again looking at the building with the bell tower and the tall wooden beams in front—only they weren't just wooden beams. Gallows. Tall and foreboding. A crow sat atop one of the gallows, eying the—my eyes widened. I quickly looked away, hand flying to my mouth. It still held a victim.

"That man was caught stealing from the merchant caravan this very morning," Sir Fern said.

Leon clicked his tongue. "Despicable."

Sir Fern nodded. "Quite so…but that's enough of that." He cleared his throat, smiling, but it didn't quite reach his eyes. "After all, the emperor is waiting, and I really shouldn't be worrying foreign dignitaries like yourselves with such…distasteful subjects."

I frowned. Distasteful was an understatement. Disturbing fit far better. But what did he just say? Foreign dignitaries? The two of us? I laughed, shaking my head. "Oh, no, actually, we're not—"

"I suppose we'd better hurry then. We certainly don't wish to keep the emperor waiting, do we?" Leon interrupted. "Sir Fern, we would be most grateful if you would be our guide." He flashed a bright smile at the red-haired man.

Sir Fern clasped his hands together around his cane. "Ah, excellent. I am more than happy to be of service—and I guarantee that both of you will enjoy your visit." He glanced back at the gleaming imperial structure. "His Excellency is looking forward to meeting the two of you. He and his mother, the empress dowager, wanted to be here and greet you in person, but unfortunately, he had a meeting to attend, and she won't be back from her travels until the day before the spring festival."

Leon shook his head. "Please, don't apologize… I'm already impressed by this show of hospitality—sending one of his own men out to greet us."

The corners of Sir Fern's mouth turned up. "You are? Ah, but this is nothing. You both are ambassadors of the most intriguing region on the continent, after all. We really should have done more for you."

Leon waved away Sir Fern's words. "Oh, no…we're simply glad to have made it here. We look forward to working closely with the emperor."

"And I look forward to learning more about you and your mysterious culture while you're here," Sir Fern said. "My Myarnan friends have told me very little about their Ivanyaran neighbors and relatives."

"Ah, I see…well, I'll be happy to answer all the questions I am able to, but perhaps you could answer a question of my own." Leon tilted his head to the side, studying Sir Fern. "Tell me, how did you know we were your guests?"

Sir Fern smiled. "Oh, that's quite simple. It was your furs, of course," he said, pointing to my coat. "Everyone knows furs like these *must* be from Ivanyar. They're impossible to get if you don't already own them." He frowned, eyes darting between us. "Well, unless they were bought with a king's ransom…or *stolen*."

My breath caught in my throat. The coat's silk fabric turned to burlap against my skin. An image of the gallows flashed before my eyes. The crow and the man's bare feet dangling in the air. I glanced at Leon, who nodded as Sir Fern spoke. Confusion fused with dread in my mind. What was Leon doing? We needed to tell this man that he had the wrong people before he assumed *we* were criminals. "Oh, no, well, actually the furs are—"

"Yes, you're right," Leon interrupted, stepping forward, in front of me. He grabbed hold of the cape, lifting it up for the red-haired man to see. "The furs are very important to our people, which is why we would never part with them for a small price."

"I see." Sir Fern's expression melted into a bright smile. He tapped his cane against the cobblestone. "In any case, shall we head inside? The emperor will be finished with his meeting soon."

Leon nodded. "We're right behind you. Isn't that right, Lia?" He nudged me in the shoulder with his elbow.

I stared up at Leon. His lips were turned up, his brows arched over his dark brown eyes. Perhaps I had missed something—or misunderstood. Surely my older brother didn't plan to fool the Vilnarian emperor into thinking we were his guests. I'd heard stories of people being executed for far less grievous offenses—like coughing in the emperor's presence. But perhaps if I spoke up before this misunderstanding persisted any further, we could be forgiven and leave the city in one piece.

I opened my mouth, the explanation on the tip of my tongue as I met Sir Fern's intense, steadfast gaze. The words froze inside my mouth.

It would be naive of me to believe in such a pleasant outcome—in Vilnaria of all places. Even if the emperor didn't hear of it, Leon and I would not be able to escape the consequences of our actions. Between Leon's words and the furs and the goods in our travel packs, they were sure to think we were like the same thieves and frauds they sentenced to hang from the gallows. To reveal Leon's lies now, would be to doom us both to death.

I swallowed hard, feeling the full strength of Leon's stare. I could practically hear him yelling for me to go along with him and his deception.

"I…yes…of course," I said, the words stumbling out of my mouth. "Um, thank you…Sir Fern."

Sir Fern dipped his head, hands clasped behind his back as he strode toward the palace's main entrance. Leon and I followed. For every step both tall men took, I found myself taking two, practically running to keep up with them.

Sir Fern showed us to the parlor, a quaint but luxurious room with flowery wallpaper. Paintings of richly-dressed nobles surrounded by wealth, warriors on horses, and various landscapes decorated the walls. Sir Fern suggested we sit down while we waited, offering to have servants take our travel bags to our guest rooms. A kind offer that Leon and I politely refused. The last thing we needed were servants going through our bags and finding the goods we had taken.

After assuring Sir Fern that we were perfectly fine with holding onto our bags, he excused himself to go find the Emperor of Vilnaria.

The parlor had been furnished with a variety of wooden, leather, and cloth-covered chairs, but I chose to sit on the edge of a small, wobbly wooden chair. Leon chose to make himself at home, sprawling out on a blue lounge chair next to a white end table. The moment the wooden door shut behind Sir Fern, I turned to face Leon.

"Leon, why would you lie to him? We can't just pretend to be other people...especially not ambassadors! When we're caught, we'll both be killed!"

Leon sighed, rubbing his forehead. "We didn't have much of a choice, now did we?"

I leaned forward, glaring. "What are you talking about? We were fine until you pretended we were the emperor's *honored guests!*"

Leon pointed to my coat. "He said he thought we were from Ivanyar because of the furs. Imagine if we'd told him he had the wrong people. He would have thought we stole them."

"But we *did* steal them. We should have turned them in the second we stepped through Eldnaire's gates, just like I said…" I ran my hand over the soft fur covering my arm, shaking my head as more strands of hair fell from my updo. "Leon, we're both going to die when the emperor comes in and realizes he was duped by two Myarnans—he might even use it as an excuse to invade!" I clenched my fists, swallowing hard. My knee bounced up and down, my heel making soft thudding sounds against the bloodred carpet.

Leon laughed, shaking his head. "I doubt this will start a war. Lia, you need to relax—"

"Relax?" I snapped, shoulders tightening, "how am I supposed to relax? If they find out that we—"

"They won't," Leon interrupted, giving me a bright smile.

I stared at my brother, digging my nails into my palms and biting my tongue to keep from screaming. I looked down at the crimson carpet, letting out a deep breath. "Leon, if the real Ivanyarans were to come—"

Leon held up his hand, smile dimming. "They won't, since they're dead. And I'm sure it'll be a while before the people back in Ivanyar even realize they're missing. It *is* over a week's journey on foot, after all." He planted his hands down on the chair, leaning forward. "And besides…this is the new emperor."

I pursed my lips, frowning. "Didn't you say that the new emperor would be exactly like the last one, or worse?"

Leon shrugged. "That was before I realized he wouldn't be."

I reached up, yanking my hair tie out and setting the rest of my hair free from the updo. It fell down to my hips, dark and limp.

"What is that supposed to mean?"

"Look, we won't stay too long," Leon said, sitting up. "We'll stay just long enough to pick up a few things, okay?"

"Pick up a few things? What do you mean—" I narrowed my eyes. "Wait, do you mean—no! Leon, we are *not* stealing from the emperor! I would *never* do that."

Leon waved away my concerns as if they were pesky gnats. "No, no...of course not. That isn't what I meant. We have an amazing opportunity here, Lia. We can get rich without having to steal a thing."

I pursed my lips as some of the tension left my shoulders. I shook my head, eying him. "Then I don't understand...what are you talking about?"

Leon smirked. "We just have to be ambassadors from Ivanyar. It's a common practice for ambassadors to be given gifts and trinkets as symbols of peace, is it not?"

My gaze drifted upward. Above Leon, a portrait hung, proudly displaying a stern-faced, mustached man wearing a crown and holding a bejeweled dagger. A shudder jolted through my body. I looked away. "No, this is absurd. Do you really think you can trick the emperor into opening up his treasury for you?"

He scoffed. "I'm sure the *Emperor of Vilnaria* has plenty to spare...and he'll want to make a good impression on the Ivanyarans by being generous."

My chair creaked as I leaned forward. "You're making a lot of assumptions, Leon," I said through clenched teeth, "but I really don't want to die all because of a couple of fluffy white furs and a stubborn brother." I gripped the edge of my chair, the smooth varnished wood pressing against my fingertips. "All of this is wrong, Lee. We can't lie…we have to stop this and leave as soon as we can."

Leon sighed. "Look, there's no other way. If we tell them what we saw in the woods then they'll think we're just making it up to save our own skins. Either way, we're going to have to lie if we want to live." His dark eyes met mine. "Just trust me, Lia. I wouldn't do anything I didn't think would work."

I swallowed, twirling my hair around my finger as panic bubbled up from the pit of my stomach. "But…we don't know nearly enough about Ivanyar to pretend to be ambassadors," I said, my voice barely above a murmur.

Leon shrugged. "The stuff Grandmother told us should be plenty."

"Grandmother may have been Ivanyaran, but she was always tight-lipped when it came to most topics. There's still a lot we don't know."

Leon grinned. "I know. No one knows about Ivanyar. That's what makes it perfect."

"What do you mean?"

He flicked a piece of lint off the arm of his chair. It fluttered down, landing somewhere on the red carpet. "Well, just think about it. We could say literally anything and no one would be able to prove us wrong."

"Leon, we can't just lie and make things up… Sir Fern said that he knew some Myarnans with an Ivanyaran background…

what if he knows a lot about Ivanyar and was just pretending that he didn't?"

Leon scoffed. "How could he? Outsiders aren't even allowed to enter their borders, and I doubt he'd know more than what our own grandmother told us. We'll be perfectly fine."

I groaned. "Leon…you're going to get us beheaded."

He smirked. "Or very rich."

I shut my eyes, clenching my fists. "I don't care about that! This is a terrible idea…it's so wrong…"

My shoulders slumped forward as a prickly sensation worked its way from the back of my throat, out to the tips of my limbs, piercing and filling me with dread.

"But…?"

I opened one eye. "I don't have much of a choice in this, do I?"

Leon shrugged. "Not unless you want to get us killed right here and now."

I stared up at the white and black tiled ceiling. "Yes, but if we fail—"

"We won't. But I can't make everything up by myself… you'll have to help too. If I'm always the one talking, they'll get suspicious. If you're going to be an ambassador, you'll have to act like one."

Three

I grit my teeth. My toes curled within my boots, and my
fingernails dug into my palms. "Leon, I think you—"

As I spoke, the door opened and a young man stepped in. He
had dark brown hair with wavy curls captured beneath a golden
band for a crown. A deep red cape flowed behind him as he entered the parlor, followed by Sir Fern.

Leon and I rose to our feet.

The emperor nearly matched Leon in height—towering over
me. I'd heard the new emperor was young, but hadn't known how
young—or attractive—he really was. Athletically built, tanned
and clean-shaven. He looked as though he could be my age, perhaps twenty-three or twenty-four. Leon and I bowed in respect.

"Please don't concern yourselves with formal customs when
we are alone. You are my honored guests," the emperor said. His
voice struck the air, carrying the weight of his authority, but he
smiled at us as if we were old friends. His gaze traveled from

Leon, to me, to the bags on the floor by our feet. "Oh, but you still have all your belongings with you… Sir Fern, will you—"

"Your Excellency…please, do not trouble Sir Fern. We've already informed him that we'd rather keep our bags with us for the moment," Leon said.

The emperor frowned. I cringed. Leon had no sense of self-preservation. Did he really think he could get away with interrupting the emperor?

The emperor looked over at Sir Fern, who raised his right shoulder in a shrug.

The emperor nodded. "Ah…of course. If that will make you feel comfortable, then you're welcome to keep your bags with you." He cleared his throat. "I understand that you have no reason to trust us at the moment. But I will personally guarantee that, as emperor, I will do everything in my power to establish a relationship between us and our nations built on trust and goodwill."

Sir Fern nodded in agreement with the emperor, his smile as warm as a mother's embrace.

No harsh words, suspicious stares, hard questions, or veiled threats. Could he really be the son of the former emperor? I clasped my hands, pulling them up to my chest.

If he knew who we truly were, we'd be nothing but worthless pests in his pristine palace. We'd be squashed like bugs and thrown out with the waste.

Leon straightened. "Your kindness does you much credit, Your Excellency. Allow me to introduce myself, I am Lyon Tynan, of Ivanyar." He turned to me, "and this is my younger sister, Velia."

I blinked. Tynan was our Ivanyaran grandmother's maiden name.

The emperor nodded. "I am Kyvir Velin Devar, and I am honored to welcome both of you to the Vilnarian Empire. Would you care to take some refreshment with me as we speak?"

He asked the question in Diarune, the mountain language commonly spoken by those in the northwest. Despite his thick accent, he spoke the tongue rather well.

Leon smiled. "We'd be delighted to, Your Excellency."

I nodded, not trusting myself to speak in front of the emperor. This man—though young—held our lives in his hand. The three men walked to the door and I followed. For better or for worse, Leon and I had entered this lion's den. All we could do now was hope the lions had already been fed.

"So, tell me about Ivanyar. What is it like?" the emperor asked, taking a sip of his tea. We all sat at a large white table at the outskirts of the garden entrance, surrounded by tall, verdant hedges which hindered our view of the garden, and flowers boasting shades of pink, yellow, white, violet, and bloodred. From behind the hedges, the sounds of rushing water and birdsong rang out.

Leon cleared his throat, as if he expected me to answer.

"Cold," I said.

Sir Fern and Emperor Kyvir laughed. I winced and looked down at my lap, my cheeks warm with embarrassment.

"My apologies, Miss Velia," the emperor said, his piercing hazel eyes meeting mine. "I wasn't laughing at you. It's simply that I didn't expect you to have such a good sense of humor." He blinked, eyes widening as he put a hand over his mouth. "I'm sorry...that's a rather offensive thing to say, isn't it..."

"It's all right," I mumbled, sliding down in my seat. "I'm not offended..."

Sir Fern cleared his throat. "In any case, I'm certain you're right about it being cold in Ivanyar."

Kyvir nodded, recovering his smile. "Your furs must keep you warm though...and they're beautiful. Is that silver thread? From Myarna?"

Leon nodded. "We get the thread there. It's both durable and decorative."

The emperor raised an eyebrow, his head tilted forward. "So... you *are* in the habit of trading? I've heard many reports that you prefer to have little contact with outsiders."

"That's true. We usually avoid spending time with strangers, but we've had peaceful relations with Myarna for decades." Leon grabbed a cookie off the plate, waving it around in the air as he spoke. "It's trust, you see. We know what goods they have to offer, and they know what we have."

Emperor Kyvir nodded. "I understand." He glanced at Sir Fern. "Well, as I mentioned in one of my letters, I would be interested in opening up trade between our two nations, if your people would be willing." He grimaced. "I didn't receive much of a response...only that ambassadors would be sent to discuss possibilities...they didn't even mention how many."

Leon frowned. "Well, establishing trade won't be easy... As I said, we've been trading with Myarna for years because of trust. Some of our people have even married Myarnans. Ties are strong."

The emperor hummed, touching a finger to his chin. "Then I suppose the only thing that would convince you to switch or open trade with Vilnaria would be competitive prices and better quality goods, correct?"

Leon pursed his lips, looking away as if he were ashamed by his country's stubbornness. The country he knew little about and certainly didn't belong to. I took a sip of my tea, reveling in the refreshing, crisp taste of mint, sweetened with honey.

"Well, yes...perhaps if my people could see some of the goods you have to offer with their own eyes...it could be enough to tempt them."

The emperor nodded. "I see... Well, I can certainly send you off with some sample goods." He turned to Sir Fern. "Please make a note. I'd like a selection of our best trade goods to be put together for our emissaries to take back with them when they leave."

Sir Fern smiled. "Consider it done, sire."

Leon sighed. "I hate to cause you so much trouble... I'm afraid even getting the council's permission to come here was no easy feat. Trust really is difficult to come by."

"No matter...the purpose of inviting you here now is to establish good relations and build up trust, so we'll start there," the emperor said, taking a small bite out of his sugar cookie.

The corners of Leon's mouth turned up. "Yes, of course, Your Excellency."

The emperor swallowed, shaking his head. "Please, call me Kyvir. I'd like to start our relations off on equal footing."

I blinked, frowning. Emperor Kyvir didn't act like the emperor of the most feared empire of all-time. No, he presented himself as a friend, with no hints of deceit or ulterior motives. Unlike Leon and myself.

We talked more as we finished our tea and pastries, but about Vilnaria—not Ivanyar. The emperor had a deep, warm voice. Whether he spoke Diarune or Vilnarian, I enjoyed hearing the emperor speak, and learning more about this empire of warriors I'd heard so much about while growing up.

"How did Vilnaria become such a large empire?" I asked.

The emperor's gaze snapped to mine. "Vil—well, my father... and my grandfather—and my great-grandfather before him, broke down boundaries and connected people of other lands, assimilating them into one nation...thus creating the Vilnarian Empire."

That was an odd way of saying they marched into territories and forced people into submission by threatening them with war and suffering, but who would want to admit that their father was a bloodthirsty tyrant obsessed with power and control?

Leon raised an eyebrow as he placed a strawberry scone on

his plate. "I've heard Vilnaria has had quite a few wars over the years."

"Well, it's mostly been small disputes that sprang up when people disagreed with authority...not full wars." Emperor Kyvir cleared his throat, placing his empty teacup back on the saucer. "Now, once again, I'd like to thank you for coming," he said. "While you're here, you will be treated as honored and esteemed guests. If there is anything that we can do to make your stay more enjoyable, all you need do is say the word and I'll see that it's done."

"Thank you, Kyvir," Leon said.

Emperor Kyvir nodded. "It's my pleasure. Sir Fern?"

Sir Fern swallowed a bite of pie, wiping his mouth with a napkin. "Right... I will be your guide throughout your stay here at the palace. If there is anything you have questions about, feel free to ask. Noon or night, I'll be available to you."

"And tonight, we'll be holding a ball in honor of your arrival," Kyvir announced, smiling.

I choked on my sugar-coated cookie.

Leon raised an eyebrow. "A ball...?"

Sir Fern beamed. "Yes, a ball! We wanted to welcome you in the true Vilnarian style!"

Kyvir looked between Leon and me. Seeing our faces, his smile disappeared. "Is something wrong? Do you not enjoy dancing? I can change—"

"No, no... We simply didn't expect such kindness from our hosts. Customs are much different in Ivanyar," Leon said, pasting a smile onto his face. "But my sister and I look forward to such an honor."

Kyvir's expression relaxed. "Ah, I see. I understand." He leaned back in his chair. "Here in Vilnaria, it's customary to host a welcome ball or party when guests will be staying for over three days."

I vaguely remembered reading something about that in a book about the Vilnarian Empire, but most of that book had been about the Vilnarian Empire and their ingenious war tactics, not their traditions for welcoming guests.

"That's an interesting custom," I said. "I do hope we'll be able to fit in well despite not being very familiar with your culture."

Sir Fern smiled. "No one expects you to be perfect, and I'll be around to help you if you should need it."

Leon grinned in return. "In that case, I'm sure we'll do just fine."

I grimaced. If only I had a quarter of my brother's confidence…

Four

I paced in Leon's room, a luxurious chamber with dark green walls, trimmed with gold leaf. A large canopy bed sat in the middle of the room, against the back wall. To the right of the bed lay a small seating area, with a brown leather couch, armchair, and small mahogany table with a large bowl of fruit placed on top.

"We should go now," I said, "end this charade. We can escape before the ball and go back to Myarna, where we belong."

Leon sat down in the armchair, shaking his head. "Even if we did leave, it wouldn't take long for them to discover we're missing and come after us. Like it or not, we're stuck here for a bit."

I pursed my lips as I continued pacing. "If we try to attend that ball, someone is bound to suspect us...we could get discovered!"

Leon sat back in the armchair. "Don't be so worried, Lia," he said, inspecting the fruit in the bowl on the table. "We're foreigners from an isolated nation. No one in their right minds would expect us to know much of anything about Vilnaria."

"But they do expect us to behave like ambassadors!"

"I doubt the Ivanyarans even had ambassadors until now."

I stopped pacing, mid-step. Leon had a point. The Ivanyarans I'd met and seen in Myarna were merely traders and farmers, not dignitaries or anything like that. For all we knew, the people they'd originally sent to Vilnaria were just three random people they'd named ambassadors.

"That's…probably true…but if we keep making things up, we're going to eventually forget what we said, or contradict ourselves…"

Leon shrugged. "We can write things down. I think there was a journal or something in the travel bags. We can use one of the empty pages to record whatever we come up with."

I turned my gaze to the three travel bags we'd dumped in the corner of Leon's room. We had yet to look at the items we'd pilfered since stuffing them in our bags. "Wait…there's a journal?"

He nodded. "Yeah, I couldn't understand any of the words though…it was written in that ancient Ivanyaran language."

My eyes widened. "Dygorin script? Grandmother taught me how to read that!"

Leon raised an eyebrow. "Can you translate the journal?"

"I can try." I walked over to the bags as a wave of relief washed over me. A written account from a real Ivanyaran would do wonders in helping us keep up appearances—and keep us from making up too many outrageous stories about their culture—at least until we could figure out how to get back to Myarna alive. Kneeling beside the travel packs, I opened one, taking the wrapped parcels out as I hunted for the journal.

"Why don't you go through this stuff and sort through it?" I suggested, glancing up at my brother. "You can pretend to be rich later."

Leon let out a long sigh but dragged himself out of his chair.

The first travel bag had no books apart from two of the five books we were supposed to deliver to the library, but the second did hold a book—the journal. The journal was covered in dark red leather, and the letter "V" had been engraved on the center of the cover.

I opened the journal, my eyes latching onto the sharp, bold strokes of Dygorin script.

The handwriting was nearly illegible, and not all the words looked familiar, but with context clues, I could piece together some of the words.

"What does it say?"

I glanced up at Leon. "Well, I think this journal was a gift... and it was definitely owned by a woman... From the look of it, she must have had this journal for a long time. This first page is stained, and the ink is smeared in a few places."

Leon shook his head, peering over my shoulder. "I think that's water damage. Must have been dropped in snow. Check how many pages she wrote in."

I flipped through the ruined pages of the journal, stopping once I reached blank pages. "Only around fifteen...you were right. It is rather new..."

Leon grinned. "Didn't I tell you? You're working with an expert, Lia. Anyway, think it'll be of any help?"

"Absolutely," I said, scanning the first page. "I just need to spend some time translating…that's all."

"Ah, well, if it's really going to be helpful, then maybe we should go back and get the others."

I stopped, staring at my brother. "Others?"

Leon nodded. "Yeah, there were a couple other journals, but since you didn't want to give up the old library books, I had to leave them behind."

I shot to my feet. "We have to go get them!"

Leon blinked, holding up a hand. "Whoa, whoa, slow it down. You really want to go back to the forest after this morning?"

As he spoke, the events of this morning returned to my mind, including the shriek of agony from the unknown woman. But this time it seemed more like a distant memory than reality. As if I'd merely dreamed it all. So much had happened since the morning. We'd gone from delivering library books to committing fraud.

I pursed my lips. "Well…if we really need to keep pretending, then we have to go…we'll need as much information as we can get if we're going to leave this palace alive."

He laughed. "I think you're being a little dramatic, Lia."

I shook my head, staring down at the journal in my hands. "If they'd send a man to the gallows for stealing from a merchant caravan, what do you think they'd do to us? Think about it…we're lying to the emperor."

Leon sighed, looking up at the ceiling. "It's fine, Lia. He's never going to find out." He clicked his tongue. "But all right, if the journals will make you feel better, then we can go get them."

I nodded as my shoulders relaxed. "All right, let's—"

"You're not trying to go today, are you?" Leon laughed, smirking. "Don't you remember? The oh-so-generous Emperor Kyvir is hosting a ball in our honor. It'd be quite the scandal if we didn't attend. I wonder…do you think the nobles who attend will give us their own welcome gifts?" My brother's eyes gleamed.

Glancing at the door, I sighed. The thought of attending a dance, surrounded by people I didn't know, twisted and turned my stomach like a baker kneading dough. "I'm not sure…"

"See, that would be amazing. The more stuff we can get, the better—faster we can get out of here, okay?"

I frowned. "…how about we don't take anything and leave as soon as we can? There's no point in adding to our guilt."

Leon shook his head. "It's a good thing we're attending the party tonight. You really need to relax and try to have some fun."

"We're not here to have fun," I muttered. "Nothing about this charade is fun." I looked down at the journal in my hands, rubbing the engraved V. "But at least we have this…"

Leon stood, walking to the leather couch, and taking a seat. "Yup. Now come on, we have about twenty minutes until Sir Fern shows up to get us to our tailors, so let's see how much we can get translated before then."

"You mean how much *I* can get translated?"

He smiled. "I'll help you by staying out of your way."

I shook my head. "Yeah…so helpful."

"Just look at this color on her! Is she not such a doll?"

The tailor's shrill squeal pierced my ears, but I stood still—stone still. With dozens of pins so close to my skin, I'd be in danger if I dared to even breathe too deep—let alone move.

Sir Fern stood to my right with his hands behind his back like an art connoisseur. He nodded in agreement with the tailor—a middle-aged woman named Alyssa. Alyssa reminded me of my grandmother. Judgmental stares and an air of sophistication, blended with a good sense of humor and a wagon load of enthusiasm.

Sir Fern cleared his throat. "Yes, you've certainly outdone yourself—"

Alyssa snorted, waving her half-rolled up measuring tape at him. "Outdone myself? Absolutely not. I just did the best I could with the material I already had. Now, if you'd warned me that she'd be the size of a child, I could have come up with a true masterpiece. But for now, we'll just have to settle for bringing up the hem and taking in the sides of the dress."

Sir Fern frowned, studying me. "I think that perhaps 'slight' or 'petite' might be a more polite description."

If I wasn't certain that even opening my mouth would end in several pins stabbing me in various places, I'd agree with them both. I got my height from my grandmother, in that I didn't get any at all. Alyssa had needed to pin up the dress just so the hem didn't lie in a pool of fabric on the floor, and the sleeves didn't swallow my arms like a starving fish.

Alyssa shrugged. "Either way, she's tiny, and I'll need to make theses alterations fast if the dress is going to be finished in time." She turned to the table, rummaging around. "Blast it all! I think I forgot my scissors..." She turned to me, grimacing. "All right, honey, you sit tight. I'll be back in a moment."

She turned, striding out the door before I could even manage to open my mouth.

Sir Fern chuckled. "And there she goes..." He pursed his lips, looking me up and down. "Miss Velia, are you all right? You haven't said a word since we entered the fitting room."

I opened my mouth, praying that I wouldn't be jabbed in the side for it. "I'm all right..." I glanced down at the violet fabric draped and pinned to and around my body. "There are just a lot of sharp objects uncomfortably close to my skin."

Sir Fern raised an eyebrow. "You and I both know that's not the only reason you're nervous."

My mouth parted, but words refused to emerge from my lips. I feigned interest in my reflection within the mirrored walls of the fitting room while Sir Fern's gaze hung on me like a ship's anchor.

"Oh, I mean...well, I've never been to a Vilnarian dance before..."

He nodded. "No, I'm sure you haven't. Tell me...do you attend balls in Ivanyar?"

"No, not exactly...we have dances that were passed down to us over generations that we perform on special occasions, and we were taught a few Myarnan dances as well." My voice trembled as I spoke. My knees shook, and my limbs were numb from standing still for so long. I glanced toward the door.

"Well, if you know any Myarnan dances then you'll be fine. Many of Vilnaria's dances are similar," he said.

My gaze snapped to Sir Fern, who smiled. I grimaced and sighed, wincing as my stomach met the end of a pin. "Ah…um, thank you, Sir Fern," I said, stiffening to avoid any further injury to my body.

His eyes flickered with amusement, "for what?"

"Your help," I said. "You've…set my mind at ease."

He studied me again, but this time I couldn't seem to discern his expression. The gleam in his eyes said that he knew something, and yet he said nothing. If he knew anything about Leon and I, surely he would have said something by this time. So what else could it be?

"I'm certain I have set your mind at ease. You've been paler than a glass of milk from the moment you arrived at the palace, and it's no wonder. You and your brother have a lot to learn." He stepped over to the table, placing something down on it.

I caught a flash of silver. "What is that?"

Sir Fern shrugged, "It appears Alyssa didn't forget her scissors after all… I simply forgot I was holding them. If you'll excuse me for a moment, I'll go fetch her."

He smiled at me before turning to walk out of the room.

Five

*E*ntering the ballroom felt like entering an entirely different country—marble floors, gilded high ceilings, and tapestries depicting historic events, like the ruination and destruction of every nation and country that Vilnaria had conquered over the last several decades.

Tables laden with refreshments lined the walls on either side of the room. Gold leaf decorated the walls, and crystal chandeliers hung from golden chains. The light from the chandeliers covered the entire room in a warm glow. We stepped forward to the edge of the short staircase leading down to the ballroom floor.

A man dressed in a red uniform stood there. He nodded as Sir Fern gave him a note. The man looked down at the piece of paper, clearing his throat.

"Ambassadors Lyon and Velia Tynan, of Ivanyar, and Sir Ferdinand of Eldnaire!" he called out as we descended down the small marble staircase.

"Everyone is staring at us," I murmured to Leon.

"Don't worry about it," Sir Fern said, glancing over his shoulder as we reached the bottom of the stairs. "They're only curious."

Leon grinned. "Yeah, we're the guests of honor, Lia. It's only natural that they'd want to learn as much as they can."

Leon wore an olive-green suit with a tan undershirt. His raven hair curled over like a falcon's talon, covering part of his forehead. After all the preparations for the ball, I felt like a princess—and looked the part. I was wearing the violet gown Alyssa had altered for me, and a few of the palace maids had worked together to do my hair and makeup. They had fashioned the top half of my ebony hair into a braided updo, leaving the other half to cascade around and down my shoulders all the way to my hips.

I wore a necklace and earrings with violet gemstones to match my gown—a gift from the emperor himself.

The gown was the loveliest thing I'd ever worn. The satin fabric was light and soft against my skin. Rhinestones and crystal beads, sewn onto the bodice and skirt, sparkled in the light. Alyssa had slit the long sleeves of the gown as if they were curtains so I'd be able to use my hands and arms during the ball. And even though Alyssa had brought up the hem of the dress so I wouldn't trip, it still brushed the floor as I walked, swishing with every step.

I glanced around the room. The musicians sat at the back of the ballroom, warming up their instruments.

"No dancing yet?" I asked Sir Fern.

He shook his head. "At Vilnarian royal events, the dancing doesn't begin until the emperor is there to lead the first dance."

I nodded. "I see…"

Leon hummed. "Well, while we wait, why don't we head over to one of the refreshment tables? I'd like another one of those strawberry scones we had earlier."

Sir Fern smiled. "An excellent idea. I'm sure Emperor Kyvir will be along shortly."

"Is everything all right with the emperor, or is it customary for him to arrive last?" I asked as we walked over to the table on the right side of the room.

Sir Fern nodded. "He's all right… He received some interesting news earlier and needed to deal with it, so he was late in getting ready for the ball. That is all."

Leon grabbed a small plate from the refreshment table, plopping two scones on it. "Oh, there's cake too."

"That's chocolate plum cake. Our head cook's specialty," Sir Fern said. "It's quite good actually. You should try it."

Leon grinned. "You don't have to tell me twice!" He surveyed the room. "Sir Fern, what's that table over there for?"

"Gifts for the two of you, actually. From the nobles."

My eyes widened as I followed Leon's gaze. Sure enough, another table stood next to the refreshments on the other side of the room. Every inch of the table carried packages of various shapes, sizes, and colors.

"Emperor Kyvir Velin Devar!" the announcer called out.

I turned. Kyvir descended down the marble staircase. He wore a dark red coat with gold buttons that shone beneath the light of the crystal chandeliers. A black cape flowed from his shoulders, the bottom of which brushed each stair as he glided down the staircase. An ornate golden crown rested upon his head.

He stopped at the bottom of the stairs, looking around the room. Spotting Sir Fern, Leon, and me, he walked over to us.

"Lyon... Velia... I hope you both are doing well," he said as he reached us.

Leon and I bowed.

"We are. Thank you for your consideration, Your Excellency," Leon said, as smooth as ever.

The corners of Kyvir's mouth turned up into a polite smile, but his eyes lacked the warmth and life they held earlier in the day. "I'm glad to hear that."

He turned to me. "Miss Velia, I'm not sure if Sir Fern has informed you yet, but the custom in Vilnaria is for the host to dance the first dance with a guest." He stared down at his hands, fiddling with them. "Of course, I don't wish to make you feel uncomfortable. Tell me, Velia...do I presume too much in requesting a dance?"

My cheeks heated up. With no reason to say no, what choice did I have other than to say yes? The emperor was just being polite—following traditions. Who was I to refuse? One dance wouldn't do me any harm.

I smiled up at him. "I would be honored to share the first dance with you, Emperor Kyvir."

The emperor's eyes widened. He cleared his throat. "Oh, the honor is all mine, of course, Miss Velia," he said, offering me his hand.

I took it, taking a deep breath. All the eyes in the room were on us, but I couldn't afford to lose focus. I was about to dance with the emperor.

The crowd parted as Kyvir led me straight onto the dance floor. My face grew hot, heart pounded—my throat tightening as the musicians started to play an unfamiliar tune. Was it a waltz or a reel? What if this was a special Vilnarian dance that Vilnarians practiced from the time they were small children?

"Kyvir…? I don't know this dance," I whispered.

He blinked. "What? Oh, don't worry. Just follow my lead." He bowed deeply, so I curtsied in return. Straightening up, he took my hand, placing it on his shoulder. Taking my other hand in his, he stepped forward, so I mirrored his actions.

He lifted our clasped hands up before pulling me into a turn. Proper etiquette demanded we have some sort of conversation as we danced, but if I opened my mouth now, I'd lose any semblance of grace. The music reminded me of a summer day in Myarna. The violins told a tale of unbearable heat, the sun's rays beating on mothers as they shopped in the marketplace. As Kyvir spun me around, the piano joined the mix of instruments, the ups and downs of the melody were like temperature changes. Pleasant in the early morning, scorching in the afternoon, and cool late in the evening.

Hearing the pattern in the music, I could anticipate which steps Kyvir would take next. When he swung me out, I swept my hand up, as if reaching for an apple in a tree. He pulled me back in, so I placed my hand on his arm.

Step forward, back, forward, twirl. The steps repeated themselves, but the music changed. The violin and piano faded, replaced by soft bells. The bells were like the children of Myarna, playing beneath the shade of trees when the summer sun grew too hot, laughing as they chased each other around the trees.

"You're smiling... A memory?"

I stumbled at Kyvir's voice but caught myself.

"Sorry, I didn't mean to scare you," he said, drawing me closer. "You were looking more comfortable, so I thought it'd be all right to say something."

The bells faded out as the piano and violins returned.

"It's all right... I was just thinking about my homeland."

He pursed his lips. "Ah, yes, I—" Kyvir stopped as he spun me around. Once, twice, and finally a third time before returning to the back and forth steps of the waltz. "Yes, I'm sure you must miss Ivanyar. I know how grateful I should be to you and your brother for agreeing to come here and meet with me."

He swung me out. I swept my hand up, bringing it back as he swung me back in.

"There's...no need for that. I'm glad to be here."

Kyvir studied me. "Are you really?"

"Vilnaria is different from what I expected...but it's not unpleasant," I said, as the music began to wind down.

Kyvir wrapped his arm around my waist, dipping me backward as the song ended. Lifting me back up, he let go of me. We stepped back, him bowing as I curtsied. Offering me his arm, I placed my hand in the crook of it.

"Would you like to go out into the gardens?" he offered.

"They're more beautiful in the daylight, but they can be pleasant in the evening as well."

With the dance over, I could feel the full force of Vilnarian stares. I nodded, smiling at him. "I'm sure they are. I'd love to see them."

He smiled in return, guiding me toward the back of the ballroom, toward the exit. As we walked, I scanned the room for Leon. I eventually spotted him over by the refreshment tables, next to Sir Fern and a blond-haired man with clenched fists and a scowl on his face.

I stopped walking. "Oh dear…" I murmured.

Kyvir glanced at me. Following my line of sight, he frowned. "That's Duke Gladik. It looks as though they're arguing."

I swallowed. "Perhaps Lyon is…well, perhaps he said the wrong thing… We're not used to the social etiquette of Vilnaria after all…and we're also not completely fluent in the language."

Kyvir shook his head. "Yes, I'm sure this is nothing but a misunderstanding." He stepped forward, gently tugging my arm. "Let's go see what all this is about."

I froze, my feet planted firmly on the ballroom floor. What if Kyvir's presence only made things worse? What if Leon had already been discovered? What if the duke had already figured out the truth? "Oh, well…I'm certain it's fine. Sir Fern is over there, and you wished to go out to the garden, didn't you?"

"Yes, but I know Duke Gladik," Kyvir said, looking at me. "Despite his young age, he's one of the most wealthy and influential members on my council. If he's displeased with your brother, he's not going to be quiet about it. Come, we should intervene."

I found myself nodding, taking quick steps to keep up with Kyvir as we walked, my gaze focused on my brother. I'd spent much of our childhood diffusing arguments between Leon and the boys he played with, before they could escalate into fistfights and brawls. I never once thought I'd have to do such a thing now that we were both in our twenties.

Duke Gladik had long, shoulder-length blond hair that hung loose around his head, and dark eyebrows. He wore a mauve overcoat, a tan undershirt, and white trousers. A golden chain connected to an invisible pocket watch dangled out of the front pocket of his jacket. As Kyvir had mentioned, he appeared to be quite young. He was shorter than Leon by about a head and a half. Even so, the duke's glower could have leveled an entire city faster than a hundred cannons.

"How dare you?" he shouted at Leon as Kyvir and I walked over. "You ignorant, uncivilized—"

"Duke Gladik, please calm yourself. You're making a scene," Sir Fern said.

Duke Gladik jabbed a finger in Leon's direction. "You, sir—and I call you 'sir' only because society dictates I should—are despicable! You're making a mockery of—"

Leon yawned loudly, interrupting the duke.

"Duke Gladik, I believe this is a party, not a court session. You are a duke, not a judge—and certainly not my mother—who is the only one I'll ever allow to scold me in public," Leon said as Kyvir and I joined the group. He smiled, "Ah, Velia, Your Excellency, how was your dance?"

"I'd suspect it was terrible if your sister is anything like you," Duke Gladik snapped.

Wincing, I could feel the color draining from my face. Ignorant. Uncivilized. Despicable. What had Leon done?

Leon's posture remained relaxed. Shoulders back, chin lifted, and hands shoved into his pockets. He even wore his signature smirk—but it didn't reach his eyes. The mischievous gleam wasn't there. I wasn't sure whether to be relieved or terrified. For once, Leon had realized that he had made a mistake.

"Duke Gladik, I must remind you that Lyon and Velia Tynan are our guests, and I will demand that you treat them as such," Kyvir said, frowning at the duke.

"Guests? No, they—"

Sir Fern cleared his throat and Duke Gladik shut his mouth, clenching his fists as he bowed his head toward the emperor. "My…apologies, Your Excellency, I know I was in err," he said, glancing at me.

Kyvir nodded. "Thank you. What happened here?"

Leon smiled, removing his hands from his pockets, placing one over his heart. "I'm afraid it's all my fault. Duke Gladik asked me about Ivanyaran culture, and my answers didn't satisfy him."

Duke Gladik glowered. "Of course it didn't! I know lies when I hear them. And you, sir, are full of them!" He turned to the emperor. "Sire, before this event, I heard from trusted sources that there is a plot to prevent good ties between Ivanyar and Vilnaria—starting with the deaths of the ambassadors traveling here. So you see, this man and his sister have got to be frauds that are here to—"

"Enough," Kyvir said, his gaze cold enough to send shivers down my spine. "Duke Gladik, you have stepped over the line by throwing out accusations against our guests with no proof. I must ask you to leave for the remainder of the evening."

My mouth dropped open.

Duke Gladik's eyes widened as well. He took a step back. "Your Excellency? But I—"

"Don't make me repeat myself, Duke."

Duke Gladik clenched his jaw. He glared at Leon and I, stalking off toward one of the exits.

Kyvir watched him go before sighing, turning to face Leon. "I apologize on Duke Gladik's behalf," he said. "Please do not allow his words to cause you offense…"

Leon's smile brightened. The familiar gleam returning to his dark eyes. "Not at all, Your Excellency. I am not offended in the least."

Kyvir looked at me. "Velia?"

I shook my head. Terrified? Yes. Offended? How could I be? The duke had told the truth. Leon and I were the ones who deserved to be kicked out. My fingers played with the beaded fabric of my skirt. "No…I cannot blame Duke Gladik. I imagine he has his reasons for being suspicious."

"Totally unfounded, I'm sure," Sir Fern said, glancing between us. "In any case, please don't let this terrible occurrence spoil your evening."

Leon grinned wide. "Spoil the evening? No, my interaction

with the duke merely made it more lively. Although, not quite lively enough. I think I'll go look for a partner to dance with."

Sir Fern chuckled. "I doubt you'll have difficulty finding one. Just about every woman in this room is holding her breath, praying you'll ask her to join you on the dance floor."

"I'd best not keep them waiting then." Leon winked before walking off into the crowd.

And just like that, he left. No genuine apologies, no consequences, just smiles, laughs, and lies. How did he do it? How could the son of a common scholar and a librarian fit in with rich nobility?

My head ached. A dull, hollow pain. Guilt poked at my stomach like thousands of tiny needles. I turned to Kyvir. "I'm sorry about all of that."

He shook his head. "Don't be. Would you still like to go see the gardens?"

I nodded, convinced that if I opened my mouth, my breakfast, lunch, and dinner would come out before any of the words that I wanted to speak. Fresh air was exactly what I needed.

Kyvir smiled. "Then let's go right now. I think you're really going to like them."

Six

*F*lickers of early morning sunlight seeped through the verdant leaves, creating small patches of light on the shadowy forest floor. I hadn't noticed before, but the forests in the Vilnarian Empire were far denser than they were in Myarna.

Leon walked beside me, scanning the forest before us. His dark eyes latched onto every shifting branch or rustling leaf. The rest of the ball the night before had gone smoothly. Kyvir and I had walked around the gardens, with him pointing out different types of flowers and trees. I wasn't able to see them very well, but I still enjoyed spending time with Kyvir.

I'd done what I could to keep the conversation on him and not me, and I learned a lot about him that I never would have guessed. His love for his mother, his passion for the people in his empire, even his fondness for plants. His gentle and patient nature surprised me. He had welcomed me into his inner world, and I was tempted to lose myself inside of it—inside of his warm hazel eyes.

If only he wasn't the emperor. If only I was nobility. Perhaps we could have developed a strong *friendship*. Of course, those thoughts were useless at best, and insane at worst. But they were still there, lurking at the back of my mind.

To think that the man wearing the crown that I'd been taught to fear and hate my entire life, had a smile that could light up the entire night sky.

The evening ended with me dancing a few more times with Kyvir, and then a couple other nobles. In the end, Leon and I may have been given wary looks, but no one apart from Duke Gladik appeared to suspect us.

Kyvir told us that we would have the morning to recover from the dance the night before, and Sir Fern would meet with us in the afternoon to give us a tour of the palace.

Though I would have preferred to spend the morning snoring away in my feather-soft bed, Leon and I left Eldnaire shortly after the sun rose, setting out into the woods in search of the Ivanyaran journals.

Despite my weariness, my mood lifted as Leon began whistling. A small part of me wanted to tell him to quiet down for fear of attracting bandits or the same murderous mercenaries that had disposed of the Ivanyarans, but instead I welcomed the distraction.

The high-pitched whistle drew the attention of several chickadees, finches, and thrushes, who hopped from branch to branch, following us as we walked.

I laughed, shaking my head. "You're certainly popular."

Leon stopped whistling, shooting me a puzzled look. "What

do you mean?"

I pointed to the birds.

Leon grinned, whistling up at them.

Their feathery little heads jerked, tilted, and bobbed from one side to the other as they chirped back.

Leon chuckled, ending his performance as the birds took off.

"From a librarian and fake ambassador to famous bird whistler...what a career change," I joked.

Leon grimaced, kicking at the ground as we walked. A few small twigs and leaves went flying, dropping back to the forest floor with a soft rustle. "I'd much rather be a whistler than stuffy bookkeeper," he grumbled. He stopped, turning to face me. "Do I look like the type of guy who belongs in a dusty old library?"

I didn't have to look at my brother to answer that question. Despite a pale complexion, his build stood solid as a stone statue. Moving stacks of books and carrying bookcases had done wonders for his physique.

I'd sooner expect to see him on a battlefield, ship, or even a throne than imagine him as a stern, scholarly, and precise librarian like our father. Although, seeing as Leon wasn't the type to take orders, being a soldier or sailor wouldn't suit him either.

I shook my head, picking up my pace. "What would you do instead?"

Leon frowned, pursing his lips. "Well, after we leave Eldnaire, I bet I'd make a great mercenary."

I stumbled but managed to regain my balance. I swallowed, blinking at my brother. "A mercenary? Like those murderers who—Leon, Mother would faint if she heard you say something like that."

"Let her."

"Leon..."

"I'm completely serious. Mother and Father might be content with staying in Myarna with their small minds and wages, but I am not." A smile formed on his face. "I've actually been thinking about it for a while now. This ambassador business is going to be just the beginning. Soon enough, I'm going to be a man of conse-quence, Lia. Money, status, respect...I'll have it all."

I shook my head, fingernails digging into my palms. "You think becoming a mercenary—a murderer—would gain you respect?"

He pursed his lips. "Mercenaries do more than kill people."

"You mean like steal, spy, fight, and hunt people down?"

"There's more to it than that." Leon sighed. "Look, Ivan has been a mercenary for nearly ten years and he's done all sorts of stuff—stuff that will make the world a better place."

My chest tightened. "Mercenaries are not heroes. They only work for the money."

He huffed, shoving his hands into his pockets. "What does working for money have to do with being a hero? Everyone needs to eat, you know... Why shouldn't I get paid for what I do?"

"That's not what I meant—"

"Lia, I can take out bandits and murderers, escort people to their destinations, stop smugglers, end wars..." He opened his arms wide. "Wouldn't you call that heroic?"

I pursed my lips, glancing up at the trees overhead. "Those

mercenaries from yesterday killed innocent people."

"You know I'd never do that."

"Yeah," I said, glaring at the ground. "Of course not."

I'd never thought my brother would steal. Never thought he would lie. And of course I never thought he'd be capable of ending lives. But how could I be sure of that after the day before?

Death was a mercenary's closest companion. It followed him like a starving dog waiting to be fed, and would not leave until it had its fill—if it ever did. Whether it would be the mercenary's victims, or the mercenary himself, death didn't care. Death had no master, only driven by hunger.

If my brother truly planned to go down this route, not even I would be able to protect him in the end.

"Huh. Looks like the campfire is still smoking."

I looked up, blinking in surprise. To our left, a murky gray cloud of smoke rose above and through the trees. The smell assaulted my senses, stinging my eyes far worse than it had when we'd first come across it the day before.

"What? Surely the campfire isn't still…there's no possible way it would keep smoking. Especially not that much…right?"

Leon shrugged. "Only one way to find out."

A familiar feeling of dread washed over me like a wave over a rock as Leon stepped off the path and disappeared into the brush. I looked over my shoulder before trudging after him.

Smoldering embers—but not from the campfire. The entire clearing looked as though someone had torched it, leaving nothing but smoke and ash. Walking closer, I spotted a partially burned leather strap. I recognized it as part of one of the Ivanyaran travel bags. I froze.

"They…burned everything…" I whispered.

Leon pursed his lips. "Yes… They did."

"Were they just covering their tracks? Why would they destroy it all?"

"I don't know, but I'll find out." Leon's eyes burned with determination. He turned, walking away from the charred remains.

"Where are you going?"

"Back to the palace," he said. "I'm going to look into this."

The smoke from the smoldering camp attacked my eyes, making them water. I blinked back tears. "Wait!" My voice came out as a strangled screech, and I winced as the echo bounced through the trees.

Leon stopped, looking over his shoulder. "What is it now?"

"How can you be so calm? So unaffected?"

Leon frowned. "What do you mean?"

I clasped my hands, bringing them to my chin as I glanced around the clearing. "The Ivanyarans were murdered, and they're trying to hide the evidence. I mean, all of this means that we're in a lot of danger, right?"

Leon shrugged. "I can't say for sure yet. Last night during the argument I had with the duke he told me he knew I was a fraud because he'd heard the Ivanyarans would be killed before they ever reached Eldnaire."

"He was right," I murmured. My vision blurred.

"Yeah." Leon shook his head. "There has to be something going on with the politics of Vilnaria that we don't know about yet."

Unable to hold them back, the tears escaped my eyes, rolling down my cheeks. "We should never have come here," I whispered, wiping away the wetness.

Leon gazed back at the charred campsite. "Don't worry about it. I'll look into this myself and figure out what's really going on."

I lowered my hands, staring at him. "Leon, what are you talking about? Forget about looking into this ourselves… We need to warn the emperor and leave Vilnaria right away. What if the duke is—"

Twigs snapped and leaves crunched somewhere far off to our right.

My eyes widened. Leon motioned for me to stay quiet, pointing at a nearby tree. He stepped over, climbing up. I followed. Reaching for the first branch, I dug my feet into the grooves of the bark, pulling myself up. Higher and higher until Leon indicated we could stop.

I looked down as two men entered the clearing. I recognized one as Duke Gladik. The other appeared to be a palace guard, carrying a halberd.

"What do you think, Duke?"

Duke Gladik bent down, picking something up from the ground. "I think I was right. Something is definitely off. This looks like a book—or at least, what's left of it."

I peered down at Duke Gladik's golden head as he walked around the campsite.

"Everything has been burned, sir. If there was any evidence of who the camp belonged to, it's long gone now." The guard poked at the ashes with the tip of his weapon.

"Yes, and I think I know exactly who did this."

"The two ambassadors, sir?"

I exchanged a glance with Leon. If Duke Gladik only knew the two people he suspected were right above him, he'd have just enough evidence to launch an investigation and heap suspicion onto our heads.

"Yes, I'm certain they're frauds. If His Excellency hadn't been so taken with the woman, he might have noticed something was off himself."

Leon smirked at me. My cheeks grew hot as I glared back. The duke thought the emperor was taken with me? No, as I kept telling myself last night, Emperor Kyvir was just that. *An emperor*. He needed to show the proper courtesy to an ambassador, which meant making certain I never lacked a partner if I desired to dance, making good conversation, and introducing me to others. There wasn't anything strange about it. It was tradition, nothing more. Regret pricked at my skin. I'd never met a man like Kyvir in Myarna. He was a good man—a gentleman—but he didn't care about me in the way the duke believed he did. I would hardly be considered a suitable candidate for a palace maid if he knew who I was.

"What should we do?" the guard asked.

Duke Gladik frowned. "For now, we watch their every move. Sooner or later, those fakes will slip up and give themselves away. All we need to do is be prepared for that moment."

"But do you truly believe they murdered the real ambassadors, sir?"

"I wouldn't be surprised," Duke Gladik shook his head. "They plan to make a fool out of His Excellency, but I won't stand for it. I'll put an end to their duplicity."

The guard nodded. "Right. For His Excellency's sake."

"We should return to the palace now," Duke Gladik said, looking around.

"Of course, sir."

The two walked out of the clearing, disappearing into the trees.

Leon and I stayed where we sat in the tree for at least twenty minutes after the two men left before climbing down.

Leon scanned the forest, nodding, "They're gone."

"Good… We should head back too."

He nodded. "The duke thinks we're guilty."

"Well, we're definitely guilty," I sighed. "But not of murder. Leon, I don't think this is going to end well."

Leon shrugged. "It's a little too late to worry about that now. We're just going to have to make this work." He glanced back. "Now, come on, the other journals are obviously long gone now."

I bit my lower lip, surveying the ashes again. "It's all gone. So much information destroyed…someone's entire life, their thoughts, hopes, dreams…their culture…"

Leon waved my words away. "Yeah, yeah, it's tragic and all that, but you know what this means, right?"

I blinked. "What does it mean?"

The corners of Leon's mouth turned up. "It means we'll just need to make more things up with the information we *do* have."

Seven

Sir Fern met us outside the palace walls, just as he had when we first came to Eldnaire.

"Ah, there you are... I heard from the guards that you left the palace. Were you exploring the city?"

Leon nodded. "It was lovely. Eldnaire is truly a wonderful city."

Sir Fern smiled. "I'd have to agree with you, biased as I am."

"I'm looking forward to seeing the palace," I said, eager to change the subject.

Sir Fern clasped his hands together. "I'm sure you are... Let's begin then." He tapped a pen against a small folder. "Hmm... where to start...ah, I know. How about the gardens?"

I smiled. "Could we? I'd love to see them in the daylight."

Sir Fern waved me off. "Of course. It's not just my job, it's a pleasure. Come, this way!" He strode off toward the side gate, which led into the gardens.

"Now, the gardens, like the palace, have in the last few years gone under renovation. Now that they're finished, they are ru-mored to be the best-looking gardens in all of the continent," he said, leading us down the cobblestone walkway.

Leon chuckled. "But I'm certain it's more than mere rumor, correct?"

Sir Fern smiled. "I'd like to think so, but some say the botanical gardens in Myarna have Eldnaire beat."

I raised an eyebrow, but it didn't surprise me that Myarna's gardens could compete with those of Eldnaire.

"Well, Myarna does carry the largest selection of biolumines-cent plants out of all gardens currently in existence," Leon pointed out. "So perhaps everyone becomes distracted by the glow."

Sir Fern laughed. "Ah, yes, surely you're right. It's the glow that attracts and lures away the minds and hearts of the people."

We waited as the guards opened the side gate for us.

"Well, here is your chance to judge for yourself." He swept his arm out as we stepped through the gates. "Welcome to the Gardens of Eldnaire!"

I sucked in a breath. Behind a hedge archway lay a grand stone fountain spurting water out of its top, surrounded by red and white roses. Farther beyond that, I could see a white lattice archway covered in lilacs, leading to a small pond filled with lilies and shaded by a large willow tree.

"Beautiful…" I murmured.

"Yeah…this is amazing," Leon said.

Sir Fern beamed. "I'm glad you think so! Now, let's—"

"Ah, so this is where our esteemed guests have been hiding."

I snapped out of my reverie, turning to see Duke Gladik. A shiver ran down my spine. The man seemed to be everywhere we went.

"Duke Gladik, allow me to apologize for last night," Leon said. "It truly wasn't my intention to offend you."

Gladik grimaced. "No, of course not… I understand."

I pressed my lips together. Nothing in his expression or tone of voice could convince me that Duke Gladik had gotten over being disciplined by the emperor.

Sir Fern cleared his throat. "I was just giving the ambassadors a tour, Duke."

"Oh, a tour? How lovely. Mind if I tag along?" the duke asked.

Sir Fern frowned. "Actually—"

"Wonderful!" The duke cut in. "I wonder… Do you have gardens like this in Ivanyar?"

Leon glanced at me. If he expected me to make something up, then he'd lost his senses. The only thing I could think of was what the Ivanyaran girl said in her journal. I blinked. *The journal*. It hadn't mentioned anything about gardens, but it did talk about flowers.

"No, uh, not at all," I said, smiling brightly at Duke Gladik.

He raised an eyebrow. "Oh?"

My smile wavered but remained locked in place. "Well, we only grow flowers native to our region, so we…don't have nearly as much of a variety as you do." It was technically the truth, but my stomach spun in circles like a fox chasing its tail.

"Ah, I see… Well, what sort of flowers do you grow?"

"Wildflowers," I blurted out. "Since they're the only flowers that can grow on the mountainside. They're...they're really beautiful."

Sir Fern nodded. "I'm sure they are. Now, shall we continue the tour?"

My hands were shaking, so I clasped them together behind my back, out of sight. With every word we spoke, Leon and I were becoming the villainous frauds Duke Gladik believed us to be.

"Yes, let's," I said, avoiding the duke's gaze.

We strolled through the garden, admiring the beauty before us. I became entranced by the colorful flowers. Myarna's gardens were truly beautiful, thanks to their many flowers and plants, imported or otherwise, but there was something different about Eldnaire. Something truly enchanting.

I admired a statue of a swan, not far from the small pond. The stone looked worn and rough. Perhaps the statue had been part of the original gardens, before the renovations.

"I challenge you to a duel! Here and now!"

Duke Gladik's voice startled me out of my thoughts. He, Leon, and Sir Fern were farther down the path to the right of the pond. I walked over, trying not to draw attention to myself. The duke's eyes flashed.

"Here and now?" Leon's lips quirked up into a smile. "Are you sure?"

Duke Gladik glared at him. "Yes, as I just said. Here and now. You will agree if you are not too much of a coward."

Leon's smile vanished. "Duke Gladik, I suggest you don't call me a coward. I was merely concerned seeing that we have no wooden swords with us." He placed his hand on the hilt of his sword. "Unless you wanted this to be a death match."

Duke Gladik frowned. "Of course not... *I'm* not a murderer." He looked around, then brightened as the fire returned to his eyes. "Very well, Tynan. We will fight with these." He stepped off the path, striding over to a tree. Stopping, he picked up a stick.

Leon stared, a vacant expression spread across his face. "A stick?"

Duke Gladik shrugged, lifting the stick into the air. "It's made of wood, is it not?"

I smothered a laugh, imagining the two men fighting with sticks like small children. Leon parrying an attack, and Duke Gladik blocking.

"This is ridiculous," Leon said, echoing my thoughts.

"This is a duel," the duke corrected. "Now choose your weapon, or concede your loss."

Leon sighed. "Fine..." He walked over to the tree, searching for a suitable stick. He picked up one about the same size as the duke's before walking back to the path.

The duke turned to Sir Fern. "Would you oversee our duel?"

Sir Fern looked as though he were trying very hard not to laugh. "Of course! I'd be delighted to. Now, take your positions."

Sir Fern and I stepped off the path as Leon and the duke faced each other.

Sir Fern held his hand up. "Ready?"

Both men nodded. Sir Fern dropped his hand.

Neither Leon nor the duke struck right away. Both appeared to be waiting for the other to make the first move. Each shifted, taking a few steps, circling each other. Leon sprang forward, swinging his stick while the duke lifted his stick to block the blow. The sticks made a solid thunk as they collided, followed by a crack as half of the duke's stick flew through the air, straight at my face.

I ducked. The half-stick landed in the flower bed behind me. I glanced at it before turning back to the duelers. Both were staring at the half of the stick left in the duke's hand. It hadn't merely broken, it had splintered right down the middle, exposing the pale, peach-colored wood inside.

Duke Gladik cleared his throat. "Perhaps sticks are not the most ideal weapons for, well…anything…"

"Why do you think we, as a society, switched to swords?" Leon said, throwing his stick at the tree where he'd found it.

"Right," Duke Gladik pursed his lips, staring at his broken stick. He sighed, throwing the rest of the stick away. "Very well, you win this time, but next time we'll have a proper duel."

"I look forward to that," Leon said, grinning.

As we returned to walking through the garden, Duke Gladik continued to ask about Ivanyar. How did we farm crops? What sort of crops did we farm? Did we pick flowers just for pleasure? What sort of animals did we farm? I answered all of his questions with as much patience and composure as I could manage.

The words—truths and lies—started to slide off my tongue like raindrops on flower petals, leaving a bitter taste in my mouth. By the time we reached the rose garden, I'd nearly built up the courage to ask Sir Fern to make the duke leave. Before I could, I spotted a familiar figure walking toward us.

Leon waved a greeting. I smiled and curtsied. Sir Fern and Duke Gladik bowed.

"Your Excellency," they both said, greeting the emperor.

Kyvir nodded in return. "Sir Fern, Duke Gladik."

Duke Gladik pursed his lips. "Your Excellency, allow me to beg your forgiveness for my actions last night. I truly regret losing my temper as I did, and I've actually joined our guests to make amends."

Leon and I exchanged a glance.

"Ah, I see," Kyvir said. "Well, if you are truly sorry, then I will not hold your actions against you any longer."

Duke Gladik let out a deep breath, bowing to Kyvir.

"Thank you for your generosity, Your Excellency."

Kyvir nodded. "Of course. Now, I was just on my way to the library. Velia, I recall that you wished to see it?"

I blinked in surprise. "Yes, that's correct."

He smiled. "Then would you care to accompany me? I wouldn't mind giving you the rest of the tour myself at a later time."

I nodded, relieved at any excuse to avoid Duke Gladik and see the library. "I would certainly enjoy that. Thank you, Kyvir."

"Lovely," Kyvir said, smile brightening. He held out his arm for me to take.

I took it, smiling at him. Leon could deal with the duke and spew lies on his own for a while. I needed a long break.

Eight

*M*y eyes widened as Kyvir and I entered the library. The ceilings were taller than the towering pines we had back in Myarna. The shelves, wide and welcoming. So many books ordered in neat rows, just waiting to be read. My heart leapt inside of me like a deer over a garden wall.

I wanted to walk through the shelves, looking for any books I found familiar. To peruse the pages of an older history book, to see if there were any notes or bookmarks still inside.

"So this is the famous imperial library of Eldnaire…" I said, staring at the view before me.

Kyvir nodded. "Does it meet your expectations?"

"It far surpasses them," I admitted. "This is amazing…"

He smiled. "Really? I'm glad. This is my favorite place in the palace."

"Oh, is it?"

Kyvir nodded. "My mother used to read to me here when I

was a little boy. It...holds a lot of pleasant memories for me."

I hummed, my fingers brushing the gold and brown spines. "I understand that... I grew up around books."

"I could tell you were well educated."

My face heated up. "Oh...you could?"

"Yes, everything about you points toward such a thing. Besides, it makes sense. You are an ambassador, after all."

I winced, glancing back at the library door. We were alone. Maybe I could stop pretending for a moment. "Well, the truth is, I wasn't actually brought up to be an ambassador," I said. "My parents wanted my brother and I to do well in life...so they saw to our education themselves."

Kyvir smiled. "I see. It must have been wonderful growing up with such devoted parents."

"It was," I agreed, looking up at the high wooden ceilings. "What a view..."

He grinned. "I've always wanted to know how it would feel to be up there. To be on top of the literary world."

Kyvir took the single step down to a lower level before offering me his hand.

"I'm guessing you have no fear of heights then," I said as I took his hand, stepping down.

Kyvir let go of my hand. "Luckily no..." his smile faded. "No, my fears are reserved for bigger troubles." He glanced at me. "My apologies. I don't mean to burden you with my thoughts."

I shook my head. "Not at all. You're an emperor...a leader. You have so many burdens that you're expected to bear alone.

I can't imagine you find it easy."

He studied me. "No, I don't. My mother and Sir Fern have been very helpful, but ever since my father died, all eyes have been on me to decide which direction I'll lead the empire."

I nodded. "Vilnaria is known for war and conquest."

Kyvir sighed, turning away. "But all I want is peace and prosperity."

"Is that really so divisive among your people?"

He let out a dry laugh as he walked over to a nearby bench, motioning for me to follow him. "You'd be surprised. A nation with a history of over a hundred years of war has learned how to profit from it."

I sat down next to him on the glossy wooden bench. "So it's in the best interests of the merchants and nobles to keep the wars going?"

Kyvir nodded. "I'm afraid that's the case."

I pursed my lips. "But what does the average person believe?"

He frowned. "Most of them don't care, or they're against it."

"Then it seems you aren't completely alone," I said, "but if the nobles want war, then I can't imagine they're happy that Lyon and I are here."

Images of the nameless figures in the forest flooded my mind. If the Vilnarian nobles had hired mercenaries to take out the real Ivanyarans, surely they wouldn't hesitate to take out the false Ivanyarans either.

Kyvir placed his hand on my shoulder. His hazel eyes exuded warmth and sincerity. "I'll do my best to protect you and your brother from the nobles, Velia. You have my word."

I smiled as my heart faltered. "Thank you, Kyvir." I looked away, clearing my throat. "So…what did you come to the library for?"

"I actually just thought I'd rescue you. You seemed rather miserable in the gardens."

My lips parted but my tongue froze. Rescue me? He could have told Duke Gladik to leave instead—or invited Leon to come along as well. What if—I cut off my thoughts, frowning. "Did I look miserable? I was trying to look perfectly at ease…"

He chuckled. "You kept looking away, or down at your feet, and you fiddled with your hands. I could tell fairly quickly that you wanted to be anywhere but around those men."

He noticed. He cared. I swallowed hard. "Oh…I see."

"If Duke Gladik made you uncomfortable, I can have a word with him," Kyvir said, "you're an ambassador and my guest, so if the duke can't show you the proper respect you deserve, then—"

"Oh, no—please don't. I'm all right!" I interrupted, leaning forward. I flashed Kyvir a close-lipped smile, clasping my hands in my lap. "There's certainly no need to speak with the duke on my behalf."

Kyvir nodded. "Very well, if you're certain." He tilted his head to the side. "Shall we look around some more then?"

We both stood and he offered me his arm, which I took before we walked off to admire the magnificent feat of architectural and literary genius.

As I walked down the hallway, I spotted Leon loitering outside the door to my room. He wore a scowl, which he directed at me as I approached.

"Oh, hey," I said, "are you done with the tour?"

Leon's scowl morphed into a glower. "We need to talk." He turned on his heel and started down the hall, entering his own room. I followed behind, lips pursed, breath held, and nails digging into my palms.

I closed Leon's door behind me as I entered his room, keeping an eye on my seething brother. "What happened?"

He whirled around. "What happened?" Incredulity filled his voice. "Did you really just ask me that?"

I frowned. "Yes…?"

He jabbed a finger in my direction. "You sold me out! Left me in the dust! You betrayed your one and only brother."

I stared at him, blinking. "Lee…aren't you being—"

"I am not being dramatic!" Leon said, folding his arms. "You walked off with the emperor and left me to suffer alone. Do you know how hard it was to deal with Sir-tries-too-hard and Duke-can't-admit-defeat?"

"I believe I can imagine," I told him, grimacing, "since you couldn't be bothered to help me when I was the one trying to deal with him myself."

Leon blinked at me. "Surely you don't intend to blame me for this…"

I pursed my lips. "I think I'd be justified in doing so. Kyvir only invited me to come along with him because he saw how uncomfortable I looked."

As I spoke, Leon shifted, straightening his shoulders as his outrage dissipated. His eyes gleamed as a smirk slowly spread across his face. "Ah, so now he's Kyvir. I knew it."

I rolled my eyes. "He asked us both to call him by his first name, did he not?"

"Not like *that* he didn't," Leon snorted. "Lia, I'm glad you're finally enjoying yourself, but now isn't the time."

"What are you talking about?"

He shook his head, clicking his tongue at me. "I'm talking about how you're over there acting like a lovesick maiden, when we have real problems on our hands."

I narrowed my eyes. "The real problems that you got us into in the first place?"

He frowned at me, crossing his arms over his chest. "I did us both a favor, Lia. Don't you see that?"

I stared at Leon—his face, his clothing. He wore a dark blue velvet overcoat with a white satin shirt underneath—a stark contrast to the simple white, tan, and brown cotton shirts and vests he used to wear when we were working at the library. His raven hair was slicked back, and he smelled of expensive cologne.

Could I continue to support Leon if he was determined to pull himself down and me along with him? Did I even have a choice? I couldn't just leave him, he was my brother after all.

"What problems are you talking about?"

He shook his head. "Let's check your room… If I'm right, then we might have a very big problem on our hands."

I pursed my lips, fiddling with the lace trim on my dress as I nodded. Leon stepped past me, opening the door that joined my room to his. He entered the room and I followed.

As I stepped inside, a shiver ran down my spine. I frowned, scanning the area. My king-sized bed stood in the corner, with all my luggage stacked neatly against the wall. The ornate carpet felt spongy beneath my feet, and the rose-colored walls created a cheerful atmosphere.

Yet something felt off. My gaze once again went around the room, finally coming to a stop on the vanity. On it sat a plate. I walked over, stopping before it. It was a plate of cookies. Chocolate chip.

"So you got them too."

I blinked. Leon's eyes were locked onto the plate of cookies.

"Too?"

He nodded, "I walked in and a bunch of stuff was off—I think someone was looking through my things—and then I noticed the plate."

I frowned. "Did you eat any?"

Leon scoffed. "Not a chance! I spoke with Sir Fern and he asked the staff, but nobody admitted to putting them in our rooms. They're obviously poisoned."

"You think so?"

He pursed his lips. "Of course. While you were off staring longingly into the emperor's eyes, I was gathering information. It turns out that a lot of the nobles are—"

"Against peace," I interrupted. "I know. Kyvir told me."

Leon raised an eyebrow. "Did he also tell you that the previous emperor—Kyvir's father—had actually planned to invade Myarna and possibly conquer the entirety of the north?"

I stared at Leon, stunned.

"The only reason he didn't go through with his plan was because he died, but what if some of the nobles still have their hearts set on the idea?"

"But...why would they want us—the Ivanyarans—dead?"

Leon shrugged. "I'm not sure yet. Maybe to get the war started? To be fair, I don't know for sure that the cookies are poisoned, but Sir Fern seemed suspicious of them."

"Then...do you think the nobles are the ones who sent us poisoned cookies or hired those mercenaries?"

"Maybe. It could be the duke."

I shook my head. "I doubt it. He may suspect us, but that doesn't mean he'd want to kill us."

"I guess not...but I wouldn't rule out the possibility."

My gaze flitted around the room. Upon closer examination, some of my belongings appeared to be out of place. My throat tightened as if someone put a noose around it and pulled as hard as they could.

"Leon, if we're in danger, we should get out of here. I mean, if our choices are leave and possibly get pursued by the Vilnarians or stay, keep pretending to be who we're not, and probably get murdered, I think I'd prefer the former option."

"Lia, we're safer here than outside of the palace. If the people who want the Ivanyarans dead see us leave, they'll probably send more mercenaries after us."

"And what's to stop them from sending them right into the palace?"

"It would be considered a midnight deal—they'd lose their protection and be tried as a common murderer or assassin if they dared attack us here."

"Are you saying we're stuck?"

"No, of course not. I just need a little more time to come up with an escape plan that'll work."

"What's so hard about that? We could wear disguises."

"True, but we won't be able to carry all the gifts with us if we do that, and that's what we came for."

"You mean what *you* came for," I corrected, "I'm not taking a single thing when we leave and I can't believe that you're still considering that."

"Well, why shouldn't I? The emperor has plenty to spare. How many nations have they plundered?"

"That's none of our business. It never has been. Emperor Kyvir wants to establish peace and he's been nothing but kind to everyone around him—even the servants."

"It's easy to be nice when you rule the world."

"What is wrong with you?"

"Me? Nothing. I'm perfectly fine—"

"You're not fine!" I yelled. Anger rose within me like smoke filling my lungs, threatening to smother and suffocate me. "You're jealous, greedy, and completely unreasonable! Our lives are in danger and all you can think about is what you can get from a man who bent over backward to ensure your happiness and comfort!"

"I'm not jealous, just opportunistic. Life doesn't give out rewards for being a good person, Lia. Maybe if it did I'd do my best to be like you…but I'm not, and I never will be."

"Leon, we have to get out of here before it's too late. We can't keep lying, and I'm not going to sit around waiting for an assassin to come knocking at my door. We have to leave or at least tell the emperor that—"

"Tell him what? That we're being threatened?" Leon shook his head. "If he tries to look into this, he may end up finding information that tells him who we really are, and I know you don't want that. It's bad enough that Sir Fern is investigating the cookie situation. We have to deal with this ourselves, Lia."

I shut my eyes, gritting my teeth. "No…we can't keep doing this. We're living a lie. Lies hurt people, and they could get us killed if we're not careful, Leon."

"You mean Lyon."

My eyes snapped open. "I said what I meant! I'm Amelia, you're Leon! We have to stop this charade… If we don't, we won't make it out of this alive!"

"You're being a bit dramatic."

"You don't have the right to say that to me."

Leon sighed. "Lia, really…"

Thoughts of how wrong this could go flitted about in my mind like poisonous butterflies. I wanted to go back—back to Myarna. I wanted to go back to the days when I wasn't afraid to live or forced to lie about nearly every aspect of my life.

And yet, against all reason, I wanted to stay. I liked living in Eldnaire. Walking in the gardens, or spending time with the emperor. I had so many opportunities. Opportunities I'd stolen from another woman. If the nameless girl from the journal were here, would she have been able to dance with Kyvir? Would he have shown her around the library? Told her things he had never been able to say to anyone else?

I would never know, but I could wonder. I could always deny the claim that Kyvir only meant to be polite and assure myself that I was special to him. But why would I? I shouldn't care. I'd only known him for a couple days.

Even so, I knew that he was kind, sweet, caring…a good man. A man that didn't live by deception—unlike me. Would he be able to forgive me if I told him the truth? Would he have me imprisoned, or executed? I knew what needed to be done, but I had put it off, terrified of the possible consequences.

"I'll tell him the truth."

Leon blinked. "What?"

I swallowed. "If we don't leave right now, I'm going to tell Kyvir the truth about us."

Leon frowned. "Now, Lia…don't be ridiculous. We can't leave yet."

I shook my head. "Our lives are in danger! What good is gold when you're dead?"

"Why can't you just trust me?" Leon snapped. "I know what I'm doing, and I'm doing it for us, Lia. So we can both live the lives we want to live!"

Lifting a hand to my face, I felt my cheeks heat up as tears pricked at the corners of my eyes. "How can you say that? Every decision you've made this far has only been for you…what you want…you've never cared about what I wanted." I shook my head as my vision blurred. "And then you tell me you're not interested in trying to be a good person…that you plan to become a mercenary—a murderer… When did you become so different?"

"Become? Lia, this is who I've always been." Leon let out a short laugh. "Does it really surprise you that I want nothing to do with books and dusty old desks? Being a mercenary means I get to travel. I can finally experience life the way it was meant to be experienced. It's the life that suits me. The life I intend to live."

I couldn't look at him. "I see."

Leon sighed. "Look, I know you don't want to break the rules, but we really aren't hurting anyone."

"What about Kyvir? He trusts us!"

"Ah, so Duke Ego was right."

"What?"

"You really do like Kyvir. More than even I suspected."

I looked up at Leon. "What? No, it's not like that. I—"

"I get that, but you know probably better than I do that it would never work, even if we weren't lying to him."

"Why would you say that?"

Leon shrugged, tapping his foot against the ornate carpet. "He's an emperor, Lia. Even if he was attracted to you, in the end he'll want some girl that would make marriage worth his while. You're better off with a mountain of gold than a guy like that."

My hands and knees shook as Leon's words pierced my heart. I let out a shuddering breath and turned away from him, tears pricking my eyes.

"I'm gonna tell him, Leon." The words left my lips in a whisper. At first I wasn't certain Leon had heard me.

He clicked his tongue. "Tell him what? The truth? No, you won't. You and I both know what would happen to us."

"Yeah, we'd probably be sent to the gallows," I murmured.

It didn't matter whether or not Leon believed me. I knew the truth, even if he didn't. I had to tell Kyvir, even if it meant losing everything.

I strode toward the door.

"Lia, where are you going? You know I—"

I slammed the door on the rest of Leon's words. My boots clicked against the gray marble as I walked down the hall. If I thought about what I planned to do, I would talk myself out of it. So I didn't. I thought of Kyvir, the man who smiled at flowers, lit up upon seeing a book he liked, and who deserved the full truth.

For him, I would give up my freedom, and perhaps even my life.

Nine

The garden sparkled in the late afternoon sunlight. Sunbeams reflected off the water in the fountains, and bees buzzed by on their way to collect nectar from within the patiently waiting petals. Hummingbirds zoomed through the air as if trying to beat the bees and butterflies to the flowers.

Yet, even with all the beauty surrounding me, somehow, I couldn't bring myself to enjoy it. In searching for Kyvir, I had found Sir Fern, who said the emperor was in a meeting. And now, I'd lost my nerve altogether.

My main concern had to do with how this would end. All deceptions must come to an end eventually. Even if I said nothing to Kyvir, somehow, the truth would be brought to light.

I could place all the blame on Leon if I wanted. After all, he was the one who insisted we take the Ivanyaran trade goods, that we lie to and deceive the emperor and Vilnarian nobles. If he'd just listened to me, we could have avoided all this trouble. But instead, I chose to listen to him. To steal with him, share in his lies, and join him in deceiving all of Vilnaria.

Now, Leon wanted to become a mercenary. To bring death and destruction upon the innocent—all for a small portion of wealth. He'd go from a deceiver to a murderer. But could I stop him? And did I have the right to? If that was what he wanted, did I really think I could come in and change his mind?

"Hello."

Jerked out of my thoughts, I looked up. Kyvir stood nearby, his head tilted to the side, studying me.

"Oh, Kyvir… Hello."

"Are you all right?"

I forced myself to nod. "Well enough…"

Kyvir pursed his lips. "Do you mind if I join you?" He nodded at the bench.

"Oh, of course…" I scooted to the side, making room for him.

He sat next to me as I watched the willow branches wave in the spring breeze and ducks skimmed the surface of the small pond.

"I heard about the duel."

I blinked. Somehow I'd almost forgotten about the childish and short-lived fight from the day before. "I apologize on my brother's behalf, Your Excellency…"

"You don't ever need to apologize for him."

I shook my head. "My brother isn't always as diplomatic as he should be. The career of an ambassador doesn't suit him well, I think."

Kyvir studied me. "Perhaps not. But what do you think would suit him?"

I sighed, turning my face up to the brilliantly blue sky. "I'm not certain…but he has his own ideas."

"Does he?"

I nodded, glancing at Kyvir. "He has it in his mind that—" I stopped, shutting my mouth. I couldn't just tell the emperor about my brother's plans, could I?

"That…?"

I shook my head. "No, it's… My apologies… I'm sorry, I shouldn't trouble you when you have enough problems of your own."

Kyvir lifted his hand, reaching for mine, but stopped short, returning it to his lap. "It's all right, Velia. You can tell me anything."

I wished that were true.

"My brother wishes to become a mercenary," I said.

Kyvir blinked. "Truly?"

"He likes the idea of the excitement… I suppose papers and politics are too boring for him."

"Boring? Even with Duke Gladik around to challenge him to stick duels?"

We both laughed.

"But I see," Kyvir said. "No wonder you're worried for him. Will he return to Ivanyar once your work here is concluded?"

I shook my head. "No…he plans to continue traveling."

Kyvir's expression softened, his eyes filling with sympathy. "I'm sorry, that must be very hard for you."

"I simply never imagined him capable of any of this…it scares me to think he'd…" I stopped, sighing. "I just want him to be content with what he has."

"I understand." Kyvir tilted his head. "And you?"

"Hm?"

"What are your plans? For when your business here is concluded?"

I frowned. "Well…I suppose…" I stared down at my lap, rubbing my hand. "I just…I don't know. I didn't really have any plans, because…I thought I'd be returning home with my brother."

"I see."

A breeze blew by, lifting strands of my dark brown hair, carrying them across my face so they brushed my cheek. I swept them back behind my ear.

"Would you consider staying, Velia?"

My eyes widened, snapping up to look at Kyvir. "What?"

He cleared his throat. "I was merely thinking. You could stay here in Eldnaire as a diplomat. Someone from Ivanyar would need to take the position eventually, so why shouldn't it be you?"

"Well…because…"

We sat on the bench, listening to the wind sweep through the branches and leaves surrounding us on all sides. Now was the time. If I let it pass, I might never have the courage to try again. I took a deep breath before letting it out.

"Kyvir… I need to tell you something."

"Yes? What is it?"

I looked over at the pond, willow, anywhere but the emperor's face. "Well, actually…the nature of this matter is…well…perhaps it's better no one should accidentally overhear."

Kyvir frowned. "Oh, I see… Shall we go to my office then?"

I nodded. "Perhaps that would be best."

"Very well."

Kyvir led me through the garden, halls, and up the stairs until we arrived at his office. As we stepped inside, I took in every detail. The bookshelves, filled with as many small trinkets and antiques as books. His desk, covered in various papers and more books.

I walked over to one of the dark leather chairs in front of the bookcase, sitting down. Kyvir sat across from me.

"So, tell me, Velia…what's the matter?"

Now that the moment had arrived, all the words I'd planned to say disappeared. I cleared my throat, staring down at my hands on my lap. Perhaps it'd be easier if I didn't have to look him in the eyes.

"Um, well…Duke Gladik was right," I said. "My brother and I aren't real ambassadors. The truth is, we're Myarnan librarians and our real names are Amelia and Leon." I shut my eyes. "I'm so sorry for deceiving you because you've been nothing but kind, and you didn't deserve to—"

"You're Myarnan?"

I opened my eyes, nodding. I couldn't detect any emotional reaction from him. "That's right…Leon and I were born there. We know a bit about Ivanyar because our grandmother was Ivanyaran, but we've never actually been there…"

Kyvir watched me, his lips drawn together. I sat up straight, ignoring the urge to squirm in my seat. The clock on the bookcase ticked—a slow, hollow sound.

"So, everything you've told us was made up."

His tone was stoic—almost calm. As if we were discussing the weather, or our dinner plans.

"Well, not everything…but yes, most of it." I shook my head. "I'm so sorry, Kyvir—"

"Where did you get the Ivanyaran goods?" Kyvir interrupted. "You couldn't have just happened to have them on hand—unless you started out with the intent to deceive us."

My eyes widened. "No! Of course not! That was never my intention… We found the goods at an abandoned campsite, and I planned to turn them over to the proper authorities the moment we reached Eldnaire but then—"

He held up a hand. "The campsite was abandoned? So you don't know what happened to the real ambassadors?"

"They were attacked…by mercenaries…"

Kyvir frowned. "What?"

I swallowed hard, staring down at the ivy-green rug beneath my feet. "Leon wanted to help them, but there were three men and I…I didn't want him to get hurt, so I told him not to…" I gripped the arm of the chair. "I'm sorry, I know we should have told someone, but I didn't know what to do when—"

"Velia—or, Amelia, you have to listen to me."

I stopped, looking at Kyvir as my chest and shoulders tightened. "What is it?"

Kyvir clasped his hands, setting them under his chin as he looked at me, his hazel eyes boring into mine. "I already knew."

I froze. The world around me spun so I leaned back, still gripping the leather chair. "What?"

Kyvir looked down at his hands. "Sir Fern told me. He knew from the beginning that you and your brother were frauds, and told me before the ball on the first night."

Staring at the emperor, everything clicked into place. "You knew the entire time...but didn't say anything?"

"I couldn't afford to," he said. "Unmasking you as fake would do no good if I couldn't figure out what happened to the real ambassadors, so Sir Fern convinced me to keep up the charade."

I shook my head, swallowing. "You knew...and yet you were so...open. So kind..."

Kyvir shrugged. "I'll admit...it was difficult. I had liked you from the time of our first meeting—before I knew the truth. But afterward, I wasn't sure how to act around you. I tried to convince myself you were a hardened con woman who would do whatever it took to take advantage of me, but everything about you said otherwise." Kyvir shook his head. "Honestly, I couldn't figure you out." He laughed, glancing at me. "The more I got to know you, the clearer it became that you didn't have a dishonest bone in your body, which confused me even more. To be perfectly honest, I'm surprised it took you this long to tell me the truth."

"Three days isn't that long..." I mumbled.

He smiled. "No, it isn't...at least, not to someone like your brother."

I winced. "I'm so sorry…"

Kyvir let out a deep breath. "Don't be. The truth is out now, and we can work together to figure this out—if you're willing."

"You don't want us to leave?"

He shook his head. "I need your help. If the real ambassadors were murdered, then I have another crisis on my hands." He shook his head, pain filling his eyes. "I should have known something like this would happen. Perhaps I could have prevented it. I'm glad you and your brother weren't harmed as well."

"There may have been an attempt… Someone left a plate of cookies in both our rooms. Leon is certain they were poisoned."

Kyvir's eyes widened. "Poisoned cookies? Why didn't you tell me about that?"

"I was going to, but Leon was afraid if you looked into it then you'd figure out who we were…"

His eyes flashed. "You could have—you both could have been killed, and he was more concerned with keeping the lie going?"

"Well, he did think that—"

A rapid knock came at the door.

Kyvir blinked then schooled his features into a serene look. "Enter."

The door opened and Duke Gladik entered, eyes alight with anger. "Your Excellency! The woman sitting next to you is a fraud!"

I smothered a laugh. The duke had certainly picked the perfect time to announce the truth. I turned to Kyvir, who gave the duke a harsh look. "Duke Gladik, did we not discuss this earlier? I will not have you falsely accusing my guests of crimes you imagine they've committed."

"But Your Excellency—I have proof!"

Kyvir blinked. "You...do?"

Duke Gladik nodded. "Yes, I knew my suspicions were not unfounded. One of the maids searched their rooms and found not only that their bags were made from a material only found in Myarna—but five books that are known to be from Myarna's library were inside of them." He cast a smug smile at me. "These people are not from Ivanyar, but Myarna. And they've been trying to fool you this entire time."

Kyvir cleared his throat. "Duke Gladik, I believe you are mistaken."

The duke frowned. "Your Excellency?"

"There were only a few things we knew about Ivanyar before our emissaries arrived to instruct us."

Duke Gladik's frown deepened. "Yes, I suppose there were, but sire—"

"One of the things we knew," Kyvir continued, "is that the people of Ivanyar traded exclusively with the people of Myarna. So would it not make sense for the people of Ivanyar to be found with goods from Myarna?"

Duke Gladik blanched. "I...well, I suppose...but Your Excellency—"

"I believe you owe Miss Velia an apology, Duke Gladik. Not only for falsely accusing her once again, but for having a maid search through her belongings. Such actions are severely inappropriate."

Duke Gladik looked like a kicked puppy. He pressed his lips together, the corners turned down. His azure eyes glistened as they darted to and fro, searching the emperor's scowling face. Kyvir cleared his throat and Duke Gladik winced. He glanced at me and sighed, his shoulders slumping.

"Ah...right...of course. You're right, of course...my apologies, Your Excellency, Miss Tynan," the duke muttered. "Forgive me for disturbing you both..."

I gave him a smile. "No, it's all right...really."

Kyvir nodded. "You're forgiven. I will see you at the council meeting."

The duke saluted the emperor before leaving the room.

"The duke truly wishes to help you," I said.

Kyvir sighed. "He'd be more helpful if he didn't get in my way."

"Why don't you tell him the truth?"

"Because he would never keep it to himself. If you haven't noticed, his moral code is rather strict."

I nodded. "Leon suspected he may have been the one to give us the poisoned cookies, but I doubt he'd do something like that."

"No, he wouldn't. Even having a maid go through your things was over the line for him. I'm surprised he'd go that far." He sighed. "In any case, I need to prepare for the council meeting, and of course, there's a feast tonight to celebrate the beginning of the spring festival, so perhaps we should discuss this more tomorrow morning." He studied me. "That is...if you're still willing to help and remain an ambassador?"

I studied Kyvir. He had to be desperate to beg help from a lying criminal. I grimaced, glancing up at the ceiling before meeting his eyes. Earnest and warm.

"You don't have to do it," he said. "You could still leave with your brother if that's what you really want."

I looked away, frowning. "I didn't tell you the truth expecting no consequences for my actions...so, if I can help, then of course I'll do it."

"Vel—Amelia, I place no blame on you for any of this."

My shoulders stiffened, "I could have stopped Leon."

"Could you really?"

I opened my mouth, only to close it. I chose to go along with him, but it would have been easier to turn night to day than stop Leon when he was determined.

"Well, either way, I want to make this right, Kyvir. I want to help you."

He smiled. "Thank you, Amelia. I hope that—" he placed his hands on the arms of his leather chair. "I mean, I'm glad that you're staying, and I'll alert the guards to watch for anyone suspicious."

"Do you believe that Leon was right? That someone may be trying to kill us?"

"I...think it's a very strong possibility," he admitted, "but I'm not going to let anyone harm you—or your brother. I'll take whatever precautions necessary to keep you—you both—safe." He stood, offering me a hand up. "And tomorrow, we'll speak with my mother about all of this."

I took Kyvir's hand, standing. "Sir Fern said she was

traveling. Is she back now?"

Kyvir nodded. "She arrived early this morning and is taking some time to rest. She was paying her sister a visit."

"Oh, I see. Well, I look forward to meeting her."

His smile widened. "Good, I'm certain she's looking forward to meeting you as well. I think she's really going to like you."

Ten

*F*or the rest of the day, I couldn't help but feel like I was being watched. I'd told the emperor the truth, only to learn that he'd known the whole time. The relief hadn't lasted long. To help Kyvir I had to keep up the charade—continue to be an ambassador. Not only was I still a fraud, but I had to worry about possibly getting murdered.

I spent most of the day in the gardens reading. I thought about going to find Leon, to tell him about my conversation with the emperor, but after our argument early that morning, I didn't feel like speaking with him. I'd need to tell him that Kyvir knew our not-so-secret secret eventually, but it could wait.

As I sat in the gardens pretending to read, I got the sudden feeling that someone was clearly staring at me. I whirled around—half expecting to see a figure cloaked in all black and ready to kill—but it was just Sir Fern. He appeared quite amused by my reaction. He chuckled.

"Whoa there, sorry, didn't mean to frighten you, Miss Velia."

I grimaced. "It's all right... I suppose I'm simply a little on edge."

He nodded. "Understandable. Near-death experiences tend to do that to a person. To think they'd use cookies..."

I blinked. "So you did look into that?"

Sir Fern grimaced. "With the help of the field mice in the barn we were able to confirm that both plates of cookies were indeed poisoned."

My eyes widened. "Truly?"

He nodded. "I'm glad your brother was wise enough to be suspicious. Don't let yourself become too anxious though, the emperor said he would protect you and he's a man of his word. He's already set up a guard to prevent any harm from befalling you."

I stared at Sir Fern. "A guard...?"

He laughed. "You haven't noticed them?"

I followed Sir Fern's gaze, spotting a guard over by a tree not too far away. I looked over to my right, spotting another. I shook my head. "No wonder I felt like I was being watched... I thought I was just being paranoid."

"No, not this time. His Excellency merely wishes to keep you safe."

My heart grew warm inside my chest. Of course, fake ambassador or not, it would look bad for Kyvir if Leon and I were killed. That didn't mean I didn't appreciate the concern though. I only wished he'd told me before I'd spent the entire morning as a nervous wreck.

The next morning, at Kyvir's invitation, I entered the apartments of his mother, the empress dowager. It looked like another palace—smaller in size—though not by much. The decor screamed *refined*. End-tables with lace and flower vases filled the halls, the walls held paintings of the empresses of the past. The carpet covering the marble floors could have been blood for how deep a red it looked.

With all the rumors and stories about the murders that took place in the Vilnarian empress dowager's estate in years past, perhaps thinking about the carpet in those terms wasn't too far of a stretch.

The maid led me to the empress dowager's parlor. She opened the door and motioned for me to enter. I did, nearly stumbling when I saw the size of the room. The "parlor" was a miniature ballroom with a black marble floor. Several crystal chandeliers hung from the gold and black gilded ceiling. At the far end of the room, a large golden stained glass window picturing a knight fighting a dragon filled most of the wall. The morning light streamed through the stained glass, casting various shades of gold on the floor and furniture.

Kyvir sat on a couch in the center of the room, across from the woman who I could only assume to be the empress dowager.

"Ah, there she is, Mother." Kyvir stood, walking over to me. He offered me his arm which I took, more than a little shocked. He led me over to his mother. "Mother, this is Amelia—currently going by Velia. Velia, this is my mother."

I curtsied. "It's a pleasure to meet you—"

The empress waved her hand to silence me. "Now, now, none of that pleasant talk. We're here to discuss more important things, so please call me Marta."

My eyes widened. The empress dowager wanted me to call her by her first name? Even if I truly was an ambassador, such a thing would be unheard of.

"What's the matter, Velia? Have you forgotten how to speak?"

I shook my head. "No ma'am…"

She narrowed her eyes. "Marta."

I winced. "Sorry…Marta."

She nodded, satisfied. "Now, sit down. We have much to discuss." She pointed to the couch Kyvir had been sitting on.

We both sat down.

"So, from what I understand, you and your brother were walking through the forest when you came across the real ambassadors?"

I frowned. "Well, sort of…they were far ahead of us down the path. We spotted them running across the road, pursued by the mercenaries."

She nodded. "I see. And you're certain they were mercenaries?"

I shook my head. "I wouldn't know… I've never seen any mercenaries before. My brother has, and he's the one who identified them." I reached into my pocket and pulled out the dragon pin which I'd brought with me. "All I know is that they were wearing brown hunting gear, and one of them dropped this pin. Apparently it's a pin Myarnan mercenaries use."

Mother and son looked at me, surprise written across their faces.

"Myarnan? Not Vilnarian?"

I shook my head, offering the pin to Kyvir. "My brother said it was Myarnan."

Kyvir took the pin from me to examine it as his mother hummed in thought.

"If the mercenaries were Myarnan, then it's possible that the ones who hired them were Myarnan as well," Kyvir said.

Marta pursed her lips. "But why would Myarnans wish to kill Ivanyarans? They're allies, are they not?"

I nodded. "Yes, we've traded with them for—" I stopped. "Of course…"

"What is it?"

I looked between them. "Myarna would stand to lose a lot if Ivanyar were to start trading with Vilnaria instead of exclusively with them."

Kyvir nodded. "I'm certain Myarnan nobles and merchants would despise the thought of losing their wealth."

"Not only that," I said, "my grandmother used to complain that Myarnan merchants would offer outrageously low prices for Ivanyaran goods. That could be what ultimately convinced the Ivanyarans to agree to meet with Vilnaria."

"I see, that's plausible," Marta said.

Kyvir pursed his lips. "But if that's the case, Mother…what should we do?"

Marta tilted her head to the side, patting the cloth-covered armrests of her chair. "I believe we need to speak to the people of Ivanyar."

Kyvir frowned, leaning forward. "Send yet another letter?

It took months for them to answer the first few, and what if it gets intercepted?"

Marta shook her head. "I assure you, it won't. Not if we have our own messenger deliver it directly." Her lips turned up. "In fact, I'm sure we can find a good solution to all our problems if we go about this the right way."

"Mother, who could we possibly send? The Ivanyarans still don't trust Vilnarians, and after they find out what happened to their ambassadors—"

"I could go." The words slipped off my tongue like a key off a broken hook before I even understood I'd said them. And now that they were out there—hanging in the air like a heavy fog—it felt right. I could go out to Ivanyar myself, to make things right between Vilnaria and Ivanyar.

"You?" Kyvir's hazel eyes searched my face. "Velia, you don't have to. We can find someone else, and you can—"

"I want to do it," I told Kyvir. "It'll help me make this up to you."

"I told you, I don't blame you, Velia. You don't need to make it up to me. Besides, you know how much danger you and your brother are in. What if—"

Marta cleared her throat. "Kyvir, if Velia wishes to help, you should let her."

He frowned. "But I—" he stopped, sighing as he rubbed his temples. "Very well. If that's what you truly want, then you can be our messenger."

I pressed my lips into a smile. "Thank you… I promise I'll do whatever it takes to make things right, if I can."

Kyvir's frown faded, the corner of his lips turned up. The smile didn't quite reach his eyes, but at least it was there.

"All right, now that your lover's quarrel is over, I need to go or I'll be late for my tea party at Lady Ellen's."

Kyvir frowned. "Mother…"

Marta smirked. "What? I haven't seen you voluntarily speak with a woman for longer than five minutes since—well, never."

Kyvir shook his head. "I have a meeting about the festival to attend."

I stood, cheeks burning. "Then I'll leave you both to your business. Thank you for hearing me."

Marta smiled. "Of course, dear. You're a sweet girl. Now, you run along and enjoy yourself. The spring festival starts tomorrow. It's one of the biggest events of the year, and just about everyone will be there!"

"Thank you… I'm sure I'll enjoy it," I said, as we all walked toward the parlor door.

A smile formed on my lips. I still couldn't be sure how this would all turn out, but it didn't look nearly as bad as it did before. Leon and I wouldn't be thrown into prison or executed, Kyvir didn't hate me, and I actually had a chance to make things right.

Eleven

*L*ater that afternoon, I sat on my bed staring at a blank piece of paper. Kyvir had asked me to speak at the spring festival the next day, so somehow I needed to come up with something to say. Easier said than done. Between my conversation with Kyvir and Marta, and my decision to travel to Ivanyar, I had a lot to consider.

As words for the speech started to form in my mind, the door to my room flew open. I let out a screech, prepared to meet my end. But instead of an assassin clad in black, Leon stormed into my room, jaw clenched, eyes dark.

"We need to leave. Now."

I blinked. "What?"

He closed the door behind him, scanning my room. "It's Duke Gladik, he has proof. We have to get out of here."

"You mean the library books and the bags from Myarna?"

Leon pursed his lips. "So he talked to you too?"

I nodded. "But Kyvir was there, and he told the duke to stop."

"Obviously he didn't listen," Leon grumbled. "Lia, he spoke to me twenty minutes ago. He knows that those library books were supposed to be delivered to the library and who was supposed to deliver them. He knows our real names, and he plans to reveal them to the public tomorrow at the festival. Everyone will know."

I stared at him. "Tomorrow?"

Leon nodded. "Which means now is the time to go."

I shrank back, my fingers curled over the cream-colored comforter spread out over my bed. "No…but I…I can't."

"What? Why?" Leon threw his arms up. "Lia, didn't you hear what I just said? He's going to tell everyone!"

I pursed my lips, still gripping the blanket. "I promised Kyvir I'd help him…"

"Yeah, well, once he learns who you really are, do you really think he won't turn on you?"

"He already knows."

Leon blinked. "What?"

"I told him right before Duke Gladik did. He already knows who we are—but doesn't intend to put us on trial—or reveal our identities."

Leon stared, running a hand through his hair. "You actually told him?"

"I told you I would."

He frowned. "Yes, but I didn't think you were stupid enough to actually do it."

"And you don't think it was stupid to steal from and impersonate ambassadors in the first place?"

Leon crossed his arms. "I did what anyone would have done."

"How could you say tha—" I stopped. Pursing my lips, I twirled a strand of hair between my thumb and index finger. "Well…in any case, Duke Gladik knowing is still a problem… Do you know when he plans to reveal our identities?"

"After your speech."

I frowned at the blank sheet of paper on my bed. "Oh… I see. So after I go up on stage and talk about the importance of relationships being built on trust and honesty, Duke Gladik will come out and expose us as frauds…" I shook my head. "I'll…have to tell the truth to the crowd," I murmured.

Leon stepped forward, placing his hands on my shoulders as he stared at me. "Tell the tru—Lia, don't you understand? Even if the emperor isn't upset with us, do you really think the same could be said of the people? They'll be furious! It'll ruin the festival—they'll riot! They'll kill you themselves! It'll be a mob!"

"But if I don't tell them, and Duke Gladik comes out with the truth, Kyvir will suffer. All he wants is peace…" I shook my head. "I can't ruin that for him."

"Then don't!" Leon snapped. "Leave now, and he can fix this however he wants to."

"I'm not leaving, Leon. I'm going to stay here and fix my mistakes," I said, voice firm.

"I'm leaving with or without you, Amelia."

I stared at my brother, recoiling. "You…would really leave? Now?"

He dropped his hands, stepping back. "If you want to go ruin your reputation and get yourself killed, be my guest, but leave me out of it."

"Leave you…out of it? Leave you out of…the very thing you got me into in the first place?"

Leon frowned. "Me? You agreed to—"

"You know the only reason I ever agreed to anything was for you!" I yelled. "I didn't want to take those trade goods… I didn't want to lie…but I also didn't want to leave you to figure things out alone." I clenched my fists. "I mean, we're siblings… We're supposed to support each other. I wanted to be there to help you get out of trouble, but now that you've gotten us both in this mess and I want to make things right, you want to abandon me. When I've never abandoned you!"

"You didn't have to come! I didn't ask for your help," he retorted.

"And yet I did help you! I've always helped you! I kept your secrets. I took the blame. I've even broken the law!" I shook my head. "Does that really mean nothing to you?"

"As I said, I never asked you to do any of that stuff," Leon sneered. "If you really didn't want to do it, you should have just said so."

Taking a deep breath, I pointed at the door.

"Leave."

He frowned. "What?"

I lifted my face, looking him in the eyes. "I said, if you're going to leave, just leave! Leave and become a mercenary or whatever lowlife position you want. Because you know what?" I jutted out my chin, glaring. "It suits you perfectly!"

Leon glared back, leaning forward. "Oh, so now you'll insult me? You're just jealous that I actually have possibilities for my life. I've never been afraid, while you're just a coward who would never get anywhere or do anything if it weren't for me!"

I sat up as straight as a fir tree. "Coward? You think I'm a coward? I'm not the one who runs away the moment my consequences catch up to me!"

"I'm not running away!" he snapped. "I'm just smart enough to know when it's time to go!"

"You're nothing but a selfish, lying, coward," I said, emphasizing each word.

Leon clenched his fists. The muscles in his arms tightened, his body shook. "I am not a coward! You're just an insecure prude who thinks she's better than everyone else just because she has some ridiculous moral code!"

His words stung like lemon juice in an open wound.

"You…you can't mean that…"

He crossed his arms, cocking his head. "And what if I do?"

I threw my arm out, pointing at the door again. "Out! Just— get out! Leave!" I practically screeched.

"I will!" Leon yelled.

He turned on his heel and left the room, slamming the door behind him.

I stared after him, trying to comprehend what had just taken place. I didn't notice my vision had become blurry until the wet droplets started rolling down my cheeks. They flowed down to my chin, where they rested like stalactites before dropping to the carpeted floor of my guest room.

Turning, I collapsed facedown onto the bed. Salt stung my eyes. My brother's betrayal stung my heart.

The next morning, I pushed all thoughts of Leon away as I searched for Kyvir. Somehow I needed to tell him what was going on—why I had to tell the truth to the crowd. But no matter where I looked or who I asked, I couldn't find him. It was as if he'd disappeared entirely. When I finally located him and his mother, I had less than five minutes before I was due to give my speech. To make matters worse, a crowd surrounded him.

My attempts to get his attention fell flat as more people swarmed around him and his mother, talking and giving them gifts. Finally, Kyvir and I made eye contact. He began walking over to me when I felt a tap on my shoulder. I turned.

"Sir Fern..."

Sir Fern smiled at me. "Hello, Miss Velia. It's time for your speech. Are you ready?"

I glanced at Kyvir, who'd been stopped by more people on his way over. "Well, I..."

"Now, now, there's no need to be nervous. I know you'll do just fine, Miss Velia."

He placed his hand on my back, gently pushing me forward. Forcing my lips into a smile, I allowed him to lead me toward the stage. I'd been too late. Now, I could only hope that Kyvir would forgive me for going back on my word.

Twelve

I looked out over the crowd, scanning everyone's faces. They all looked excited. As if they truly looked forward to hearing me speak. Perhaps they did. I forced my grimace to morph into a smile.

"Hello, everyone. It is a pleasure to stand before all of you today. Staying in Vilnaria has been an amazing experience for me. It's only been a few days, and yet I've already learned so much about a culture very different than my own." I smiled. "Your emperor is a wonderful man. His desire for peace has been such an inspiration to me." I took a deep breath. "And because of that, there's something I have to say…"

As I spoke, my eyes fell upon Kyvir and a man I'd never met before. They walked over, stepping up onto the stage. Without a doubt, the man stood taller than Kyvir and my brother. Like Leon, his shoulders were broad and his arms had more muscles than a tidal pool. He wore a thick fur cape and boots made of black leather. His long, dark hair had been pulled back out of his face, drawing attention to the scar on the center of his forehead. With the white fur cape resting over his broad shoulders he looked more like a mountain than a man. He had to be an Ivanyaran. A *real* one.

The audience noticed my attention shift and several of them gasped. The stranger joined me at the front of the stage, smiling.

"Mind if I say a few words?" he asked in the mountain tongue.

I nodded, unable to take my eyes off him.

The Ivanyaran man turned to address the crowd.

"Hello, my name is Kay. I am from the nation of Ivanyar. It's a pleasure to meet all of you."

With those first words spoken, he'd already captured the attention of everyone, including me. Eloquent and gentle, I, along with everyone else, hung upon his every word as he spoke to us about Ivanyar.

He explained how Ivanyarans harvested their crops—in the warmer months, how they used light crystals to cook—just as I'd guessed. Every word Kay spoke confirmed my lies. I stood there on stage, trying not to show my shock.

"I'm sorry I was not able to make it to Vilnaria sooner, but I do appreciate your willingness to welcome two of our own." Kay looked over at me, smiling again.

I blinked in surprise. He was covering for us?

"I look forward to seeing how our two nations can work together to create a new future," he continued, "one beneficial for us all."

The crowd clapped and cheered as Kay grinned and saluted

them. Kyvir joined us on stage.

"People of Vilnaria, there you have it, the future of Ivanyar and Vilnaria, is one to be built upon peace, not bloodshed. We shall be allies. Friends, ready to turn to each other in our times of need. Trade shall be established, bonds forged. With this agreement created, a new era will start, and Vilnaria and Ivanyar will prosper."

The crowd's cheers grew louder, only calming as Kyvir prepared to speak again.

"In a few days, we shall bid farewell to our Ivanyaran friends for a time as they start their journey homeward to make contact with their people and discuss trade deals. But this goodbye will not last forever. In time, we shall see them again." He smiled. "This isn't the end, but the start of something wonderful."

Kyvir and the cheering crowd saluted each other as he ended his speech. He turned and nodded to me and Kay before walking off the stage. I followed, dazed. Ahead, I spotted Sir Fern.

I froze. Next to Sir Fern, stood Leon. He met my gaze, the corners of his mouth turning up in a smile.

I rushed forward, passing Kay and Kyvir. Upon reaching Leon, I pulled him into a hug.

"You came back..." I murmured.

"Actually, I never left."

I pulled back to look at him. "You didn't?"

He shook his head. "I, uh...well, I was angry, and I packed my bag, but I also thought about what you said, and you were right... It was sorta my fault you got involved in all this."

I raised an eyebrow, stepping back. "Sorta?"

"Hey, is this your apology or mine?"

I rolled my eyes, but a smile sprung to my lips. "You still haven't changed."

He grinned. "Why would I do that? I'm perfect just the way I am."

"Excuse me, did I miss something?" Kyvir asked.

I cleared my throat, brushing a few loose strands of hair behind my ears. "Right, my apologies." I turned to Kay, looking up at the mountain of a man. "It's nice to meet you," I said, keeping my voice low. "Thank you for your help."

The mountain—Kay—shrugged. "Don't thank me, thank the emperor."

I looked over at Kyvir. Handsome and impeccably dressed as always, Kyvir wore a black suit-vest with a light green undershirt in honor of the spring festival. "Right...well, thank you, Kyvir. How did you manage to set this up?"

Kyvir blinked. "What?" He held his hands up, shaking his head. "Oh, no...I don't deserve any credit. Actually, Sir Fern is the one who spoke with Kay."

My gaze turned to Sir Fern, who smiled at Kay. "Kay here is an old acquaintance of mine," he said, "he's actually from Myarna."

I frowned. "From Myarna? Then how did—" I stopped, gaping at Kay. "Wait, you're not really from Ivanyar?"

Kay laughed, glancing at Sir Fern. "Ah, no, not at all... I'm simply a Myarnan with Ivanyaran relatives. Like you."

I shook my head. "I never would have guessed."

He gave another mountainous shrug, hand on hip as he looked down at me. "I could say the same for you. It's no wonder you and your brother were able to fool everyone."

Before I could respond, I spotted a familiar figure heading our way. Duke Gladik.

He stopped before us, bowing deeply. "Miss Velia, Mr. Lyon, my deepest apologies for the way I've treated you... I see now that I was very wrong to mistrust you, and even more wrong for the way I've dug into your private affairs. I dare not ask for forgiveness for the dishonorable way I've conducted myself, but I do wish for you to understand how deeply regretful I am of my actions."

I blinked. Once, twice, a third time.

"Duke Gladik, thank you for your apology, I am more than happy to forgive you," Leon said, smiling.

The duke nodded. "Thank you. Your forgiveness is an honor I don't deserve."

As the duke spoke, I felt a light tap on my shoulder. I turned to see Kyvir offering me his arm. "My mother will want to speak with us."

I smiled, taking his arm. "All right."

Nodding farewell to the men, we walked a short distance away to meet with the empress dowager, who stood beaming like the afternoon sun.

Marta pulled Kyvir into a hug before turning and giving me the same treatment.

"Excellent work, dears," she said as she pulled away, smiling at us. "I'd say that speech was a success. The people now desire the peace you spoke of, and the nobles will have no choice but to acquiesce."

Kyvir nodded, letting out a deep breath. "That's my hope, but only time will tell if this plan will work."

"Either way, we're off to a great start." Marta glanced at the crowd the guards were keeping from getting too close to the royals. "So, why don't the two of you go and solidify it?"

I frowned. "What do you mean?"

Marta chuckled, lowering her voice. "I'm sure you'll think me to be rather forward for admitting this, but when Kyvir first suggested we invite Ivanyaran ambassadors to Vilnaria, I told him it would be a good idea to seek a romantic relationship if possible."

As if time itself froze, I stood like one of the statues in the royal gardens, gaping at the former empress.

"These sorts of situations are best resolved with a political marriage," Marta continued. "It gives the people a reason to root for peace—outside of moral and altruistic reasons."

My head spun faster than the wheels of a runaway wagon rolling down a hill.

"But I… I'm not…"

Marta laid a hand on my shoulder. "I know you're not really Ivanyaran," she murmured, "but I think this situation can be resolved in a way that is beneficial for us all." Marta took a step back, grinning. "Besides, I can easily see the two of you falling in love at some point in the future."

Kyvir coughed. "Mother…"

"You know I'm right, son," Marta said, glancing at him. "Either way, it couldn't hurt for the people to see how close you both are, so why don't the two of you go ahead and greet them—seed the idea of a future engagement?"

Kyvir frowned, looking to me. "Velia, you don't have to do this."

"Would you...rather that I didn't?"

His eyes widened in surprise at my question. "What? No, that's not at all what I was suggesting. I simply don't wish for you to feel obligated to do this."

I smiled up at him, despite the army of invisible spiders crawling around in my stomach. "Then...why don't we do as your mother suggests and go greet your people?"

Kyvir's shoulders relaxed. A smile lit up his face as he offered me his arm. "Very well, let's go."

"Would you like to head back to the palace? We could walk in the gardens..." Kyvir suggested as we walked.

"I'd like that," I said.

After standing and talking to a countless number of people, I was just about ready to collapse right where I was. But the promise of a quiet and peaceful walk among the shrubbery didn't sound at all unpleasant. Especially if it meant that I'd have the chance to speak to Kyvir alone.

Kyvir nodded as we began the walk back toward the palace,

escorted by guards. As we walked, people waved and smiled at us, some even saluted in respect for their emperor.

When we finally reached the gardens, I was more exhausted than I'd been from traveling all the way to Vilnaria from Myarna.

We entered through the gate, and I relaxed upon seeing the familiar beauty of the garden scene. Flowers swayed, blown by the breeze beneath the bright afternoon sun.

I glanced over at Kyvir. He was smiling as his gaze drifted from flower to flower, tree to tree, fountain to fountain. I took a deep breath before letting it out.

"So…Kay?"

Kyvir looked at me, letting out a short laugh. "Oh, yes…Kay. I'm sorry I didn't tell you about that earlier, Velia. We only came up with the plan last night when Leon told us what was going on."

My eyes widened. "Wait, Leon went to you?"

Kyvir nodded. "Last night. That's when Sir Fern revealed what he'd planned."

I pursed my lips, looking over at the rosebushes surrounding one of the larger fountains. "I truly thought I was going to have to tell the truth—without letting you know beforehand."

"You were prepared to paint yourself as the villain who deceived me?"

I nodded, "Yes…"

He shook his head. "Well, fortunately, that wasn't necessary."

"No…but I'm still living a lie." I sighed.

"It won't last forever."

I let out a breath. "Yeah…I'm going to fix this."

Kyvir pursed his lips. "You truly intend to go to Ivanyar?"

"I do."

"I see…" he smiled. "Then I wish you the best of luck. I'll do all I can to help you—I give you my word."

I nodded. "And I will return…for you—if that's truly what you want."

He tilted his head. "What?"

I turned, studying his face. "I'm going to return here, Kyvir, and when I do, I'm going to make things right. I'm going to show everyone who I truly am, and if they will accept me then I would love to consider a future here with—"

I stopped as Kyvir placed a hand on my shoulder. He leaned toward me. Bending over, he pressed a kiss on my forehead.

Thirteen

Two days later, I found myself in my room, packing my bag. Kyvir had council meetings to attend, and paperwork to sign, but he had still made time to speak with me whenever he could. I also spent a lot of time with Marta and Sir Fern, having tea and listening to them swap stories about Kyvir or their own lives.

I smiled as I folded up the dress Alyssa had created for me, placing it in my travel pack. A reminder of the first ball I'd ever attended.

"So…you're going to Ivanyar?"

I jumped, glancing up. I relaxed upon seeing Leon leaning in the doorway to my room.

"Yeah, I'm going to fix this mess for them."

He smirked. "And then come back and marry the emperor?"

My face heated up as I recalled everything Marta said. "We just met, and we're not in love."

"But you will be eventually, I'm sure."

I hummed, stuffing more clothing into my travel pack. "Who knows?"

Kyvir and I had never actually spoken about what his mother had said, only hinting at it, and perhaps it was better that way. Neither of us were ready for a decision like that. Kyvir still had to prove himself as emperor, and I needed to bridge the gap between Vilnarians and Ivanyarans. After that, we'd just have to wait and see what happened between us.

"Hey…do you maybe…want someone to accompany you?"

I stopped mid-shove, looking up at Leon. "What about becoming a mercenary?"

He shrugged, eyes on the floor as he traced the designs on the carpet with his foot. "I mean, there'll be plenty of time for that afterwards…" He pursed his lips. "And, I guess I did kinda get you into this mess, so I might as well get you out."

Abandoning my travel pack and unpacked belongings, I stepped over to him. "You're serious about coming?"

"Yeah, if you want me to."

I looked away, hiding my smile. "Well, yeah, I think I'd like someone to come with me."

"Just someone?"

"Well, I'd certainly prefer it if my older brother came." I glanced at Leon. "Have you met him? He's good with a sword, smart, reckless…and terrible at getting out of trouble."

Leon shook his head. "He sounds like an idiot."

I slapped a hand over my mouth, smothering a giggle as I nodded. "Yeah, he definitely is," I said, tilting my head. "But you know what? He's pretty great too. And skilled… He was trained by a mercenary, you know."

Acknowledgments

A huge shout out to Michaylah Malone. You were the first person to read this story when it was written. Thanks to your help, it's improved a *lot* since then.

I'd also like to thank Brad Pauquette for not only seeing potential in this story, but encouraging and helping me to see *The Librarian's Ruse* through to publication.

To Lindsey Backen, I'd like to thank you for your phenomenal copy editing skills. You saved this book from *many* grammatical errors.

Alli Prince, thank you for *all* the work you've done. Between assisting with the copy edits, designing the book's layout, and proofreading, you've helped so much!

And though we've never met, I'd like to give a big thank you to Jessica for designing the cover.

I want to give a special thanks to those of you who read and reviewed *The Librarian's Ruse* or posted about the book on social media.

And to Mom, Dad, and the rest of my family and friends who have been supporting me every step of the way, thank you. Without you, this book never would have made it to print.

Thirzah

Thirzah was born in the Netherlands, but grew up in Southern Maryland.

In her spare time (what's that?), Thirzah enjoys hanging out with other writers, creating jewelry, and making fantasy maps.

As the managing editor of *The Pearl* (pearlmag.co), Thirzah has worked with many writers to help them improve their work.

Learn more about Thirzah and connect with her on her website, ThirzahWrites.com, and find her on Instagram @thirzahwrites

*Help other readers find books that they'll love by
leaving an honest review of this book at
Amazon.com or Goodreads.com*

Don't stop now!

More great stories are just around the corner.

New short stories posted weekly.

100% free. 100% good. All the time.